Pr

Jinwar and ~~Other Stories~~

MW00475056

Poppe's finely-observed, well-turned stories of soldiers, expatriates, and immigrants cast light on an aspect of the American experience that oft eludes literary notice: namely, the toll and echo of its recent imperial misadventures.

—Marc Edward Hoffman, writer and critic,
The Nation, Bookforum, Al-Monitor

Alex Poppe is a writer with laser eyes and a scalpel for a pen, a savvy, sometimes cynical sometimes screaming inside worldly artist who tells, with her heart, the stories of multiple modern women, from the hip, savvy Xanax addicted former soldier, raped by her commanding officer, who works in a VA hospital and then a hot dog stand, to a young woman and her aunt in the land of Saddam Hussein, ISIS, the Pesh Merga, and the Kalashnikov, to a pregnant young Arab and Israeli soldiers, to the Oakland Public Library.

Poppe does not waste a word. She makes you care about and root for each woman you meet. She doesn't write to make you feel good but shows you the truth. She is edgy, off-kilter, smart, lovingly vulnerable, and searing in her descriptions. When you feel only despair she ends with the power of love. Every man who thinks he knows the world should read this book, as well as every woman.

—Jere Van Dyk,
The Trade: My Journey into the Labyrinth of Political Kidnapping; The New York Times, National Geographic, CBS News

Alex Poppe delivers an outstanding collection of stories delving into the lives of deeply powerful, lovable, courageous young women and how their lives are shaped in the aftermath of war. Captivating, poetic, weighty—Poppe's writing demands to be read.

—Hannah Sward,
Queenie Goes to Bosnia and Other Stories; Strip

Alex Poppe's new collection *Jinwar and Other Stories* is a knife in the groin, a secret stash of Xanax, a Kalashnikov in every car seat. But it's also a butterscotch sunset, a harpist at a bus stop, a chocolate truffle pressed into a survivor's palm. In locales as divergent as Kurdistan and Oakland, hot dog trucks and VA hospitals, Poppe delivers lucid and convincing characters, women and girls who are constantly defined by the way others see them yet refuse to settle within those limitations.

Whether dealing with the aftermath of violence, the trauma of dislocation, the hypocrisy of religious zealotry, or all of the above, these characters share a simple desire that is too often thwarted: autonomy over their bodies and their futures.

Like the characters in her stories, Poppe's sentences move like "a caged bird who wants her home to be the sky," ducking and rolling to avoid the confines of the page, soaring like they never want to come down. This bracing collection reminds us that in a world ravaged by war and violence, refuge can take many forms, but is regularly found in portions as small and potent as a story.

—Jeremy T. Wilson,
Adult Teeth, Nelson Algren Award

These stories bring the world alive in rich detail. They resonate forward. Each new event seems to turn a corner that leads to an unexpected laugh or jarring irony, or sad surprise; we don't see it coming and then, there it is—inevitable, true. Poppe's prose is wickedly sly; sturdy, starchy, shocking. Her sharp insights about people are placed within cultural juxtapositions that are often hilarious. The stories are ripe with surprises as weird as life.

—Ellen Kaplan,
The Violet Hours, Images of Mental Illness on Stage

The paradox at the heart of the *Jinwar and Other Stories* is that while Alex Poppe brings us into worlds of utter desolation, a VA hospital, the bleak regions of northern Iraq, the occupied territories and the shattered lives of woman struggling in the wake of sexual and emotional violence, she does so with so much lavish and lyrical attention to the sensual world, that the physical world may be all that is left of solace.

From the torture facilities of Saddam's Iraq to a hot dog food truck during Weiner Week, Poppe's fierce unsentimental intelligence and exacting eye for detail lift what might otherwise be utter desolation to something approaching resurrection.

—Joel Hinman,
Director of The Writers Studio, New York

For Pete

Jinwar
and
Other Stories

Alex Poppe

 Cune

Jinwar and Other Stories
by Alex Poppe
© 2022 Alex Poppe
Cune Press, Seattle 2022

Paperback ISBN: 978-1-951082-05-5

Library of Congress Cataloging-in-Publication Data
Names: Poppe, Alex, author.
Title: Jinwar and other stories / Alex Poppe.
Description: Seattle : Cune Press, 2022.
Identifiers: LCCN 2021008199 | ISBN 9781951082055 (paperback)
Subjects: LCSH: Women--Fiction. | Women--Abuse against--Fiction. |
  Syria--History--Civil War, 2011---Fiction. | LCGFT: Short stories.
Classification: LCC PS3616.O6568 J56 2022 | DDC 813/.6--dc23
LC record available at https://lccn.loc.gov/2021008199

Credits: Calligraphic design in "V" (pages 83-89) is Basmalah (Thuluth Round) from the IslamiClip Calligraphic Designs #1 collection by Mamoun Sakkal. Cune logos (including series logos) are by Mamoun Sakkal: www.sakkal.com

The "Credits" portion of this Copyright page is continued on page 126.

 Aswat: Voices from a Small Planet (a series from Cune Press)

Looking Both Ways	Pauline Kaldas
Stage Warriors	Sarah Imes Borden
Stories My Father Told Me	Helen Zughraib

Syria Crossroads (a series from Cune Press)

Leaving Syria	Bill Dienst & Madi Williamson
Visit the Old City of Aleppo	Khaldoun Fansa
The Dusk Visitor	Musa Al-Haloul
Steel & Silk	Sami Moubayed
Syria - A Decade of Lost Chances	Carsten Wieland
The Road from Damascus	Scott C. Davis
A Pen of Damascus Steel	Ali Ferzat
White Carnations	Musa Rahum Abbas

 Bridge Between the Cultures (a series from Cune Press)

Confessions of a Knight Errant	Gretchen McCullough
Afghanistan & Beyond	Linda Sartor
Apartheid is a Crime	Mats Svensson
The Passionate Spies	John Harte
Congo Prophet	Frederic Hunter
Music Has No Boundaries	Rafique Gangat

Cune Cune Press: www.cunepress.com

Table of Contents

Jinwar

Part 1

Sunlight streaked through the orange-red leaves, illuminating the dust motes hiding in the pale air. Bridget, the student nursing aide supervisor, was helping a chubby toddler feed the ducks in the artificial lake at the center of the grounds. Her gentle cooing skimmed over grass blades and floated up to the window, where I stood. My forehead was slick with a layer of oil. My scrub top was crusty with dried oatmeal, and my pockets were bloated with wadded Kleenex. Visitors' Day was winding down. On Visitors' Day, we got a lot of extended family and clergy and shiny people who came because the other people who came were shiny and felt guilty, and no one was too ashamed to cry big tears, and stay for a few hours to feel good about themselves and the time they had just put in, and they needed extra Kleenex from the student nursing aides who were always there.

I watched Bridget skip across the soft lawn to deliver the child back to his mother. Like me, the mom stood apart, watching Bridget and her son. Beyond clarifying the intricacies of patient sponge baths, I never spoke to Bridget. We were separated by experience and by the fact that she pitied me. Bridget was twenty-four, which was four years older than I was, and we had spent every weekday of the autumn here. I did it because I was addicted to Xanax. Bridget did it because her brother was still deployed, and she believed that her helping someone over here would increase the chances of someone helping him over there.

Bridget swung the toddler high before placing him at his mother's empty side and nodded towards the window as she walked back to the main building of the VA hospital. The mother bent down to retie her son's sneaker laces and her skirt rode up, revealing a dancer's legs. I left the freshly cut grass smell of the open window and entered the Clorox air of the linen closet to check my stash, pausing to grab an alibi of bleached sheets. Bridget, trailing sunshine, passed me as I exited and crooked her finger for me to follow. Over her shoulder she told me there was a Teaching Point, a new patient, still unconscious from surgery, and we needed to monitor his vitals as he had just lost both his legs from the hip down. I didn't ask what'd happened to his in-between.

She entered room 308 and led me into the stale dark. A fraction of a man lay in the bed. An endotracheal tube snaked past a faint harelip scar above his upper lip into his mouth, and even though his eyes were closed, I saw that this head and torso belonged to my ex-commanding officer. I stepped into the bedside table and knocked over a silver-framed photograph of a beautiful mini-skirted woman with ballet legs holding a baby upright against her chest for the camera.

I'm sorry, I said. I was sorry I had said sorry.

Bridget's face wrinkled through a chain of causality. If A leads to B, and B leads to C, then A results in C; after which she said nothing, as if to say, Can you handle this? with an element of, You'd better handle this because he and others like him have sacrificed so much, so that you and I can stand here with our whole selves fully intact, so I said, It's okay, to mean I'm okay, I can handle this and so much more, so please continue to instruct me.

The next day was the start of Marine Fest, a three-day bacchanal during which thousands of marines would arrive and celebrate being marines in our very stately and very gracious town. On the last night of the festival, when the marines were decked out in their best Blue Dress "A"s, sipping cocktails in the Potomac Ballroom Library to celebrate the 239th birthday of the Marine Corps, I would be cleaning bed pans of loose stool because during that day and the one before, able-bodied marines would have visited their disabled half-bodied brethren and snuck them tastes of all they had been denied. During my rounds, the visiting marines would tell me to take extra good care of their boys, and they would laugh fatly as if to say, You are here to service, or they would wrap their fingers around my wrist as if to say, I could break you; except for those marines who exhaled briskly through their teeth as soon as they stepped back into the hallway. Those marines would slip me a fifty and say thank you with their eyes glued to their shoes and I would wonder at their imprudence and give the fifty to Dr Bob, a fourth-year resident with a gambling problem and a liberated prescription pad. Dr Bob lived in a high rise near the marina and claimed to know what every nursing aide tasted like.

Bridget knew about Dr Bob but couldn't do much. She was small and Christian and dyed her hair blond and kept two extra pairs of ironed scrubs in her work locker so she could change if a guest had an unfortunate accident. She called the patients guests because she felt it added an element of optimism to the VA. The VA was very clean and very cold. Bridget led seminars on

Turning and Positioning, and kept an eye on us. Most nights after her shift ended, she headed to the hospital chapel to log in a half-hour of prayer for the worst-offs. I overheard her tell an unconscious guest she did it to stock up brownie points with the Man Upstairs, and would be happy to put a word in for the mummified man in the bed before her. She couldn't control the nursing aides in their free time, but she could make them clean bed pans on her time. All of the nursing aides did yoga and were blond and had Botox. Once a month, they pitched in and bought some black-market syringes of filler and bribed a cosmetology technician to smooth their foreheads or plump out their lips and hands. Afterwards they'd hit Chihuahua's to sip frozen margaritas through extra-wide straws.

Dr Bob rolled five marijuana cigarettes for a twenty in the dry-goods storage room behind the cafeteria in the basement, which is where Bridget would find us on the night of the Marine Corps Birthday Ball, and she would be in an uncharitable mood that evening because some of the marines who celebrated the Corps' birthday every year, a group of dog trainers for the Corps and not actual combat soldiers, husky, and raucous and braggadocio drunk, had cornered her by the hospital gift shop and sung her the Marines' Hymn with altered lyrics and Bridget had to smile like a girl unwrapping an expensive present she knew she was getting and shuffle over in her regulation shoes and thin cotton scrubs to shake each enormous calloused palm and gush You are our heroes! You are our heroes! and let the handshakes turn into full body hugs while each marine took his turn feeling her up. When Bridget found Dr Bob and me lying across plastic-wrapped cartons of adult diapers smoking a joint, she would have some things to say about my blackened soul and some more things to say about my degenerate character, which was worse than a gutter-tramp's, and only one thing to say about the prospects of my future training as one of Her Certified Nursing Assistants.

But this shift was winding down. I'd spent the last bit of it sitting with the patients who hadn't had any visitors, watching reruns of *The Price is Right* and betting on the over or under. Lance Corporal William Philips won a new car and my Caribbean cruise vacation in the Showcase Showdown, which made him happy because an ambush in the Anbar Province had taken his sight, so he didn't drive anymore. I fluffed his pillows during the commercial break and folded his fingers around a chocolate truffle because I remembered when I was a kid how excited I was when someone paid me a bit of special attention just because. The truffle was wrapped in fancy foil with a famous quote printed on the inside. When we were little, my sister had a desktop calendar with a fresh aphorism printed on each page of the year. Lying shoulder to shoulder on our stomachs with our bare feet dangling off the edge of her twin bed, we'd look for meaning in the convoluted words. We'd look for significance in anything, we wishers upon eyelashes.

The truffles came from a store-within-a-store inside the hospital gift shop. They were sold by Sonny who'd spent four years in a federal penitentiary for drug smuggling, following seven years on the lam. A DEA officer spotted him in the background of a Bud Light commercial, which is how he got caught; and then a local church organization led by a former New Orleans Saints' cheerleader thirty years past her prime organized a petition drive, which is how he got out early, two years ago at age seventy. Sonny often asked me how I could eat so much chocolate and still be as skinny as dripping water. He'd ask, Where do you put it? In my pocket, I'd say, and this much was true, so I didn't say anything else. He'd tsk his tongue against the roof of his mouth, but put a few extra pieces in my bag. People who knew about Sonny's past compared him to Gene Hackman, and I think he liked that.

I righted the silver-framed photo, which still had its worn price tag stuck on the back. My ex-commanding officer was my ex-adjudicator and had signed off on my discharge without benefits. He was once a strong and beautiful man. His wife, probably his wife, entered as I was recording his pulse and respiration rate. I say probably his wife because, although he wore no ring, and had never had at the School of Infantry, Camp Geiger, she did. The two-carat solitaire caught the last rays of sunlight streaming around the edges of the blinds covering the window. I figured this ring to be a neon announcement of worth, a quantification to the world of how much she was loved, and I felt sorry for her, and for myself, to be caring for my ex-commanding officer here, in this place of broken people, and for her to see that her handsome husband was now a half-man, and no amount of prayer or medical miracles or stored up good deeds was going to restore the other half. She was in a lose-lose situation because if she stayed with him, she would grow to hate him and if she left him, she would hate herself, at least for a little while, and if she stayed and had an affair, then all his comrades-in-arms would hate her, unless the affair was with a fellow marine that her husband had pre-approved. In the right now, she'd need a robust mental Blu-ray collection because he would never again be with her in that way a man is with a woman, similar to but not the same as the way he was with me, which was why I was no longer part of the Marine Corps. I was an excellent misjudge of character; this ability was, in part, why a year ago I was nursing broken ribs and a bruised back at the Camp Geiger infirmary.

I was standing with the patient clipboard against my chest. The wife slid into the spouse-spot on the window side of the bed. Bridget was watching to make sure I didn't upset her or anything else in the room, and I thought about excusing myself so I would not have to watch the wife's fragile shoulders move up and down like creased wings, but marines are taught to suck it up and move forward, and if I left now, Bridget would think I was delicate, and she had little regard for me as it was.

Bridget offered to check on the wife's toddler, who was probably being fed chocolate fudge brownies from the Get Well Soon! baskets that piled up in the nurses station, to give her some moments alone with her husband. Because Bridget regarded me as an extension of herself when she was teaching, I returned the clipboard to its naked tack and prepared to leave. But the wife blinked with incomprehension so I doubted she equated the still bundle in the bed with her understanding of husband. She introduced herself as Ashley and said that we should stay, she didn't wish to inconvenience us, and we should go about our business as if she weren't there. Then she told us what good people we were to be doing what we were doing, and because I don't like to talk, Bridget said thank you and regifted her praise to all the men and women in uniform who serve this great nation and to God, who always got praised by Bridget in case he was listening. I don't think Ashley was on speaking terms with God because that's when she interrupted Bridget with a snorting cough and turned her eyes on me, looking at me for a long moment. Bridget followed Ashley's stare to the trail of dried oatmeal dotting my shirt and suggested I excuse myself to change my scrub top.

I nodded at Bridget's advice and exited. I didn't want to feel sympathy for Ashley. I didn't want to fold her jeweled fingers around truffles wrapped in inspirational foil because she had been loved and cherished by my ex-commanding officer and he had broken me. I walked past the nurses station where their son was sitting on a desktop boxing with a Tweety Bird balloon tied to a gift basket handle. He cried Duck! every time he hit the bird's face, and it arced low to the floor before coming back for more, and the little boy would laugh a sound like splashing water.

Bridget probably knew I didn't keep an extra scrub top in my locker. No abandoned shirts lay on the changing room floor. I rubbed at the dried oatmeal with some wet paper towels, which shed a layer of soapy paper dandruff along the institutional green-colored cloth. Standing in my bra to wash my shirt in the sink, I imagined how Bridget and Ashley's patient-care conversation would go:

New trainee?

Yes.

Any good?

No.

Think she'll improve?

Probably not, bless. But God never gives us more than we can bear.

I visited Lefty, an artillery gunner who liked when I read to him. We were working our way through *Something Wicked This Way Comes* when Bridget stopped by his open door and beckoned me. Bookmarking our place with a truffle, I laid the paperback beside his pillow and told Lefty I would see him later. When I stood, Bridget pursed her lips at the wet patches on my uniform top.

I thought I told you to always have an extra uniform at work.

I forgot.

Do you know the new patient?

I bent down to pick up some invisible lint so I would need to wash my hands. My scrub pants were too long, and the place where the hem dragged on the ground was outlined in a gray. I straightened and crossed to the sink. Over the sound of running water, Bridget recycled her question.

Do you know him?

No.

Bridget checked Lefty's chart and exited. I followed about half a pace behind.

I'll need to pray for him tonight.

Yeah.

After you do a bed pan check on the floor, you can go.

Okay. Great.

Are you going out tonight?

I don't know.

You've still got slop on your shirt. Since you're not going out, you'll have plenty of time to launder and press *two* fresh shirts for your next shift. I want to *see* them before you go on the floor. Am I understood?

Yes, I said. I wondered if Bridget was going out after her all-inclusive chapel stop and if she had any friends either. Even though she meant well, in her own way, the other nursing aides kept their distance. Bridget was pretty in that conventional style that women found reassuring and men found non-threatening, so she'd probably never had a locked and loaded .45 held at the base of her skull as someone older and of a higher rank pulled down her pants against her will and made her cry. I could imagine Bridget marrying one of the charity cases in wheelchairs, an officer candidate friend of her brother's, someone with a short life expectancy and a generous pension payout, some-one who told blond jokes and could not fuck his wife but actually liked women.

I went into the supply closet where I kept my stash. With the door shut, it was colorless and quiet inside, and I liked it because then I was just a person in a supply closet in a hospital. My fingertips grazed the stacks of starched, clean sheets, some of which were rough and some of which smelled like a Chinese dry cleaner's. From my stockpile of Xanax, I slid an orally disintegrating tablet under my tongue and waited for my blood to stop crackling and for my con-scious mind to settle into that zone between drunkenness and consequence. I took only half the dosage, in case I ran into Bridget again, and stored the other half inside my bra cup.

∿

To the bed pans. In Staff Sergeant Mohammad Aksari's room, a lively poker game was in full swing when I came in. Staff Sergeant Mohammad Aksari was a career officer with seven tours of duty split between Iraq and Afghanistan under his belt. Many of the marines who cycled in and out of the VA had served with or under him, and he was popular because of his knowledge of Arabic and his commitment to the Corps. He sat in bed with his knobby potato toes sticking out from under the blanket. Sometimes when I gave him a sponge bath, he'd tell me to do my duty and suck him off. I'd say, *khabir,* which I thought meant dick in Arabic but which I later learned meant expert. The poker game cloaked me in invisibility so I left his bed pan where it lay before marking zero output on his chart and slipping away.

Dusk had shifted to stars. From room 308's doorway, I saw that Ash-ley had gone, maybe to take her son home or to get something to eat, so I entered. The room felt womb-like. In its soft opacity, my ex-commanding officer looked as dignified as he had on that first day of School of Infan-try training. In the corridor, footsteps were ushering the full-bodied outside, back among the living. The headlights on their cars were guiding the drivers away from the VA hospital, probably towards the marina. At midnight, there would be amateur fireworks you could watch from the promenade. This was in anticipation of the Corps' birthday. It was part of the town's effort to make the visiting servicemen and women feel appreciated in a world grown weary of war. Since my discharge, I had been living in a nearby beach town, renting a room from a medicated bipolar heiress who dabbled in interior design and was a devotee of face yoga. When her parents divorced early the next year, and her father's new girlfriends began refurnishing his many residences, she would find herself out of a decorating job and move to Los Feliz to try to break into stunt work. She'd try for movies, and then for television, and then for commercials, and finally for computer games. I'm still waiting to see her Claymation head being decapitated from her anatomically-enhanced body when I play *Assassin's Creed* on my Play Station. I would like something big to happen for her because she never said a word when I sampled from her bathroom's well-stocked medicine cabinet, and particularly because on the evening of the Corps Birthday Ball, when Bridget discovered my prone body across boxes of adult incontinence products, Dr Bob at my side and his joint in my hand, and after clearing out my locker and being escorted off the premises, I would arrive home to an empty apartment with full pill bottles which I'd empty, and because the emergency medical technicians smelled marijuana on me, they'd call the police who'd search the house and find my roommate's hidden cache which I hadn't known she had, which would make this the last autumn she lived in this beach town.

I settled into a chair in the corner of the room and marveled at where my ex-commanding officer's legs used to be. He had practiced martial arts and used to deliver a mean roundhouse kick. This man, my former commanding officer whom I would have risked my life for once upon a time, was so still, so motionless that I felt a certain grief. Because he was no longer the Man In Charge, he no longer owned the truth.

We'd met on the first day of School of Infantry classroom instruction. He epitomized the ideal marine: courageous, honorable, committed. He told me what to expect during the twenty-nine-day Marine Combat Training Course and promised to impart the knowledge and ability necessary to operate in a combat environment. He made me feel at home and said he'd show me the ropes to get me qualified. Later, he spoke to me privately about not wearing makeup around the other recruits or running in jogging shorts because some marines viewed the women on the base as walking mattresses who were there only to be fucked, and I would be asking for it if I did either of those things because who doesn't capitalize on an opportunity that's presented to him, and

I didn't want to be charged with conduct unbecoming did I, and to remember that boys and girls and alcohol just don't mix and from that point on only he would be able to sign off on my qualifications and I should come to his barracks for those signatures. I might have sneered a little, I don't know because I can't control it, and in times of great tension or danger I sneer.

That's when he started sleeping in my bed. I'd come in from training to find him sprawled across my mattress, and then I'd have to wait inside my car, which was the only place he didn't have a key to, until he woke up and went away. When I finally reported him to the higher-ups, I was asked if I had a boyfriend and was told that I was weak to complain about him just because I didn't like him. One of them suggested I was a hot little mess who was trying to destroy the Corps, and maybe I should be tested for a personality disorder.

The door to the room opened. I should have jumped up and pretended that I was doing something other than sitting in the semi-darkness with a rehearsal corpse, but the Xanax had kicked in so I didn't. It was Miss Patty, the Tex-Mex floor nurse who was on husband number five and therefore impossible to surprise. It's bath time, was all she said, and then, Give me a hand. I filled a small bowl with warm, soapy water and gathered some supplies. Miss Patty leaned over the bed and pulled my ex-commanding officer towards her. Get the tie, she said.

I didn't want to get the tie because then I might touch him, and I didn't want to see a spread of flesh that was both strong and weak at the same time, and I didn't want to be close enough to smell his dead-weather smell, but I got the tie because that is what student nursing aides do, and more important, that is what marines do, and it wasn't as bad as bringing him his coffee after he kicked my legs out from underneath me when I had gone to his office to retrieve the supply closet keys so I could feed the station dogs as part of my nightly cleanup duty at Camp Geiger. Miss Patty gently laid my ex-commanding officer back against his pillows, then drew the gown up past his shoulders and chest. There wasn't much left of the area below his belly button. The part that wasn't covered in plaster and bandages looked like it had been through a shark attack. Tiny beads of perspiration formed above my upper lip and I used my lower lip to wipe them away. OK, Miss Patty said, but she was looking at me, then OK Handsome, and she was looking at him, We're going to give you a little spa treatment so you can rest more comfortably during the night, even though he wasn't conscious to hear her, and then she sponged at his face, neck, chest, and arms as one would a newborn. I took away the damp used cloths and gave Miss Patty clean ones before I rolled my ex-commanding officer onto his side so Miss

Patty could clean his back. I was surprised he seemed as heavy now as he had then, when he had used his body to pin me down on the barracks' floor, because there was so little left of him. Is there anything else you need me to do? I asked and when Miss Patty shook her head I exited into the mall-lit hallway.

Ashley had just stepped off the elevator and was walking towards my ex-commanding officer's room. Oh, you're still here, she said but she didn't sound surprised, to which I said, Yes, and then we stared at each other like two people who don't know each other and therefore have nothing to say. The whites of her eyes were hacked by tiny broken blood vessels. Well, I said and took a step around her, which she countered with, Wait, and then, I am so sad, which was said so quietly that I wasn't sure if it had come from her or me. I took a truffle from my pocket and held it out to her. This might help, I said. When she didn't respond, I explained, There's an inspirational message on the inside. Ashley didn't take the candy so I added, It tastes good too, and then lifted her left hand from where it hung at the side of her body and formed her fingers into a tiny cup. It might help with the sadness, I said as I dropped the chocolate into her palm and closed her fingers around it. I turned and walked away because I had just lied to her. Nothing eased the sadness.

Thank you, she said as she caught up to me. You must be tired after such a long day. Would you like to have some coffee? I told her I didn't drink coffee and needed to get going, which was another lie because there was no one and nothing waiting for me anywhere. She opened her mouth to say something but her words got caught in her throat, which made her face look like a fish. I smiled at this, and she must have taken my smile as reconsideration because she closed her mouth and swallowed and looked at me the way a pretty child looks at the new kid before she invites her to play. Then she said she would like, if it wasn't too much trouble, for me to sit with her in the hospital cafeteria while she worked up the nerve to enter her husband's room. She said she had asked me because she could see that I was a kind person, a good person, a person her husband would like, and my giving her the truffle had confirmed this. I kept my face very still, and tried not to think, as I followed her into the elevator and we stood side by side silently watching the floor numbers light up in descending succession, about what her husband might say if he knew his wife had decided to confide in me, or if he'd worry that I might share a few secrets too, or if any of what he'd done to me had affected his life at all.

I sat at an out-of-the-way table as Ashley stood in line. At this late hour the cafeteria was almost empty, and most of the kitchen staff were smoking cigarettes in the alley beside the delivery dock as they played Frisbee with their hair nets. The place stank of tater tots. The church bell ring of glass shattering against linoleum tile pierced the chicken-fried air. A litany of Spanish swear words rang out from the dishwasher. Across the fluorescent bulb dining room, Miss Patty momentarily lifted her head from the romance novel she was reading and then sipped discreetly from a black chrome flask she kept tucked away within her ample bosom. She flexed and pointed her toes, which were propped up on the chair across from her. My stomach growled. I unwrapped a chocolate. *An eye for an eye leaves the world blind,* is what the wrapper read, which was said by Gandhi, which figured. I crumpled it into a ball and shot it across the table at the bottom of Miss Patty's feet as Ashley returned with a coffee and a bottle of water. In case you change your mind, she said as she placed the water in front of me and slid into the adjacent seat. Thanks, I said but I didn't mean it.

I don't know why but I'm afraid to see him, she blurted.

Because you don't want to face what your life has become, but I didn't say that. Instead I said that it had to be hard.

You must see patients like him all the time. Does it get to you?

No, I said and for the first time I told her something true.

How not?

I lay the bottle of water on its side and spun it on the table.

Why do you work here? Do you have family in the military?

My father was a Chief Petty Officer and my grandfather retired as a Sergeant Major. Where was your husband deployed? I didn't tell her that the last time I had seen him was at Camp Geiger.

He went to Afghanistan seven months ago, she said, twisting her diamond ring along her delicate finger, as if to say, You made me a promise, but not so forcefully as to say, You betrayed me; obviously you can't be trusted; obviously you failed me and your country.

C'mon, I said as I stood, Let's go. It won't get any easier.

We stopped shoulder to shoulder outside room 308. Do you want to go in alone? I asked, to show her she couldn't back down.

No, she said, Could we enter together?

OK, I said as I opened the door and gave her a little, hard shove forward. I hung back as she approached my ex-commanding officer. His body added contour to the upper two-thirds of the bed, while the lower third of the bed was flat.

Ashley stood in the spouse-spot shaking her head.

What, I asked, but I did not go to her.

He doesn't look like himself, she said.

I wanted to laugh a little, but I didn't.

It's the facial hair. He would never let himself go like that.

This much was true. I had never seen him look less than recruitment poster-ready, not even when he grabbed his loaded .45 and chambered the round inches from my ear.

Do you think we could shave him?

I imagined holding a sharp blade next to his jugular.

Do you think you could show me how? Are you trained to do that? The wife asked.

I'm trained to do that, I said. I raised the head of the bed so my ex-commanding officer was in a seated position. Imagine if he had awoken right then. Imagine his surprise. I could not look directly at his face, but I thought about holding the skin under his jaw firmly and tightly as I ran a razor along it. I need to get some supplies, I said as I turned toward the doorway.

I exited.

I walked down the hall past the supply closet to the stairs.

Once inside the stairwell, I sat down on a step and pressed my sticky forehead to the metal railing. Then, I extracted the other half of the Xanax from my bra and placed it under my tongue. I waited for a while, during which I am sure Ashley found another nurse's aide to gather shaving cream and towels and a razor, and show her how to shave her half-husband.

I took the stairs to the garage park and headed for my car. As I was fumbling for my keys among truffle wrappers and used Kleenex, I heard a familiar God-praising voice. I ducked down between my car and the next, just as Dr Bob strolled by, ruffling Bridget's hair and then cupping her behind.

You did good today, he said.

Part 2

The sun was high above the river, and a great blue heron was hunting for fish in the shallow water. Its mouth startled open as a dragonfly alighted upon its long orange bill and crept forward, gossamer wings gently grazing the heron's white face. The heron's eyes crossed inward, before it jerked its head and swallowed the dragonfly whole. Wayne, Jed's son, was layering sauerkraut and spicy horseradish on his foot-long hot dog, using an open potato bun as a plate, and keeping a side-eye on me, because he liked to act like he was in charge or maybe because his father had told him to. A thick film of salt had gathered behind my ears. My work shirt smelled of fry oil and onions, and the waistband of my jeans was gummed to me with sweat. There'd been a game earlier. On Game Day, we got a lot of families and bros who came to the hot dog truck because dogs and tots taste better when you're drunk, and no one was too embarrassed to stumble across the gravel parking lot and pee into the river.

I noticed an old man in shorts, socks and sandals shuffle towards the food truck, picking his ear. He, too, was watching the heron stab its sharp bill into the river to retrieve a fish, drops of water glistening like sequins off its S-curved neck. Wayne farted, a long dry, rancid rip and then inhaled deeply as the heat inside the truck intensified his tang. I specifically loathed him, partly because he idolized Jed and partly because he was fourteen, which was eight years younger than I was, and we had spent every weekend of the summer together working inside a sauna-ed, hot dog truck—on the weekdays when he was at summer school, I worked with Jed or occasionally Shenetta—I did it as part of my probation, and Wayne did it to "learn the ins and outs of business, son" and do his part to "Make America Great Again." I'd arrive at Jed's house, where his wife Maryann made me wait outside as Wayne finished his breakfast, and then Jed would drive us to whatever festival or summer camp or VA hospital he deemed Ready For Dogging! Because Jed liked to monologue when he wasn't listening to Fox News, I rode in the rattling tin truck alone or with Shenetta. Wayne always sat in the cabin with his father, on soft-cushioned seats, in the air conditioning, where men could be men.

Wayne nodded at me as he shoved three tater tots inside his mouth and then panted hot air past his yellowish, buck teeth. I fastened a smile to my face and turned toward the food truck window as I took out an ordering pad and pen and got ready to pretend to care. The old man pulled his finger from his ear and inspected it before wiping it against his shorts and then rested his elbow on the food truck window ledge. With his eyes still on the menu board, he ordered a Chicago Dog, and I saw that this man was my ex-counselor. I bumped the Hot Diggity! condiments dispenser on the service counter and sent a shower of snot-colored relish onto his dalmatianed arm.

Sorry, I said, when I wanted to say fuck.

He gave me the narrow-eyed look you give a counter girl if you're the kind of person who thinks service people are stupid, and I watched his face go through a type of prayer: God grant me the serenity to deal with the idiots of this world, the courage to maintain my self-control, and the wisdom to cover my tracks if I don't, after which he said, It's okay, as if to say, God, give me strength, you clumsy, good-for-nothing; and then, Jesus wept. It's you, with an element of Is this what's become of you, then? After all the time and energy I put into you?, and I said, Thank you, to mean Your hard work paid off, and Yes, although I am standing inside a hot dog truck shaped like a giant wiener, I'm off Xanax, so please feel good about your guidance during therapy. I held out a napkin.

The next day was the start of Wiener Week, a subsidiary celebration of National Hot Dog Month, a five-day excuse to savage-eat, during which thousands of graduates from the American Meat Institute would arrive and share tips on how to avoid sauce slippage when scarfing down chili dogs. Paper trash would confetti the parks and fairgrounds in our very antebellum and very hospitable town. On the last day of that week, I would have a line of customers which wrapped in crop circles around the hot dog truck, and I would mix up the vegetarian and meat fry oil so the churros tasted like beef eclairs and the hot dogs were tinged yellow-brown, and nobody would eat before a fifty minute wait, and since there was nowhere to sit, some people would get fed up and leave before they had picked up their orders and their stinking, greasy food would pile up and attract every cockroach swarming in meat casings to feast upon the error of someone else's impatience. Some of the Yelp reviews tweeted from the comfort of bars with huge ceiling fans and grand seating would give us no stars, to say You should have crawled back inside your mother's hooch, or gave us a half star, to say You are a waste of space; except for those people who were former wait staff and would therefore give a five star review, commenting on how hectic the night was and that we had done the best we could under the circumstances, as if to say how much working behind a counter, any counter, but especially the counter of an infernally hot phallic symbol, is mostly an exercise in remaining calm. I would wonder about them, about how their lives had progressed from Behind The Counter, and if any of them believed true life transformation was possible at all. Jed did, with the help of Our Lord and Savior, Jesus Christ, and when he read those reviews, he would feel egregiously aggrieved and blare Fox News in the truck cabin while he had Shenetta crouch below the steering wheel and suck him off until he came. Shenetta was a light-skinned, mixed-race single mom with a very dark daughter, and sometimes when folks saw them getting ice cream together at Cold Stone Creamery, they asked each other why a white woman would want to steal a black child.

Jed would laugh heartily at this and sway a bit upon his heels outside the truck next to the *The Dog Wagon* sign. The sign featured a plump, red-brown hot dog, its casing tied off in the shape of a cat's asshole, snuggled between two halves of a bun. The bun doubled as the body of the wagon, each white wheel on the sign bulls-eyed with a red hub. Delta Kappa Epsilon boys like to pose in front of the sign with their hands cupped under the wheels for Instagram photos. On days when the weather was mild, Jed stayed outside the truck talking to customers about bologna facts and how to prevent hamburger sweat stains from forming under his armpits. He was middle-aged and pot-bellied and losing his fair hair, and he wore a red MAGA cap to hide that. He thought the cap recalled his glory days of playing baseball with the Lynchburg Hillcats—he sometimes swung a roll of plastic wrap like a baseball bat before he swatted Wayne on the behind—but in reality, it made his face look too big for his head. Jed concocted the day's specials from whatever toppings were about to spoil. He kept the toppings in an extra, family-size refrigerator in his garage. I'd watch him sniff at plastic containers or double-dip his pinky finger into random sauces for taste tests. His pride and joy was The Intimidator, a half-pound all-beef hot dog slathered with blue cheese, hot buffalo sauce, crushed jalapeno potato chips, and chili, which he usually served on Fridays. That's when he'd get together with the other hot dog kingpins, a posse of fly fishing, deer hunting, Pabst Blue Ribbon beer drinking Trump voters and play pick-up soft ball games against the fried chicken franchise owners at the lighted field near the river. Once a week, they'd eat their Intimidators and then head to the softball diamond, where they'd belch out poultry insults at the other team's batters and count down the innings until they could go home and take a massive shit.

Those were the nights Shenetta read tarot cards for voluntary donations behind the fry oil containers attached to the back of the truck. Jed scorned this behavior as un-Christian, saying it and the people who practiced "that voodoo crap should go back to their huts," but in the end he couldn't do much. Shenetta was curvy and knowing and had a lilting voice which she never raised, and when she got angry, she grew sloe-eyed, and the person she was angry at soon suffered some mysterious misfortune. Some townspeople swore she had the sight, and they would line up for curly fries and a chance to cheat fate. The night Shenetta read my cards was the night that the US senators announced their intentions to confirm Brett Kavanaugh as the newest Supreme Court justice despite credible sexual assault allegations and his temperamental and unhinged testimony. Jed and his goon squad, self-righteous and re-masculated and more than a little drunk, were jubilating over the Senate's decision, running victory laps around the hot dog truck, high fiving and clapping one another on the shoulder shouting, No Mob Rule! and Four More Years! when they found us sitting on opposite sides of a lit candle with the tarot cards turned face up. Jed pulled Shenetta to her feet and made her dance to the music playing inside his head while one of his cronies stumbled over the candle, setting the tarot cards on fire. Shenetta's eyes darkened and slanted at him as the third goon hauled me over his shoulder like a dead deer carcass and spun. We both fell down, me punching him wildly until Jed pulled me off, him with a face like an exploded hot dog. Once everyone was disinfected and bandaged and re-liquored and calmed down, Jed would have some things to say about how sin was too stupid to see beyond itself and how sin always wounded the sinner and that there was no room for sin in his Hot Dog Haven, so as much as it hurt him, he was going to have to let me go.

But this shift was almost done. I had spent most of it listening to a download of Dr Christine Blasey Ford's testimony on my phone in between debating the merits of food on sticks with Wayne and asking customers if they'd like to super-size their disco fries for just a dollar more and reminding them to save some room for chocolate or caramel churros unless they preferred key lime cake. And if a customer had debated with himself or me about which hot dog toppings to get and if Wayne wasn't looking, I would sneak a side of the toppings he had not chosen into his hot dog box even though he hadn't asked because I knew how much I appreciated when someone did me a favor just because, which was partly why I was inside a hot dog truck and not an institutional facility. When Dr Ford explained how neurotransmitters code memories into the hippocampus so a trauma-related experience is locked there, I took my ear buds out and dumped all the contents of the Authentic

New York Red Onion Sauce jars into a foil to-go container so I could de-crust the ridges on the tops of the jars and under their lids.

That's my side work, not yours. Wayne's front teeth gave his face a rabbit quality.

So.

You still have to do yours. I'm not doing it.

I know. I put my ear buds back in as Dr Ford was explaining that indelible in the hippocampus was the uproarious laughter, her perpetrators' laughter, the laughter of two friends having a really good time with one another at her expense while she lay trapped beneath one of them, and that was what she would never forget. Taking a plastic knife, I chipped at the caked red-brown gunk scabbing the jar lids and Wayne went back to evaluating how fat or ugly the people walking by the river were.

It's easier if you soak them, Wayne said as the plastic knife tip broke off and flew into the Hot Diggity! condiments dispenser.

I know, I said, as I got another plastic knife. I didn't hear laughter. I heard the cli-click of a round fitting a chamber.

My ex-counselor took the napkin, which promptly tore as he wiped at the splattered relish. A few more, please, he demanded without looking at me. I reached under the counter to retrieve a Wet One, which we sometimes used to clean the deep fryers when we ran out of dish soap, and thought about Dr Ford's collegiality, which, at first, I thought made her cooperative but later I thought made her a victim. Thank you, my ex-counselor said, taking the moist towelette, and then So? To which I said nothing, preferring to hear the pigeons off the river softly coo rather than a pack of feel-good lies shuffle out of my mouth. He turned his attention to the river bank where a tall and beautiful man was running, and a husky was trying to mount a Jack Russell sniffing the grass.

My ex-counselor had been court appointed as part of my rehabilitation after my suicide attempt thirteen months prior, so every day for the six months I lived in the group home, I sat in a circle with other people who found it painful to exist in this world as a closeted, divorced man propagated the joys of living. How much longer for that Chicago Dog? he asked, not taking his eyes from the runner. About ten minutes, I lied, embarrassed to be serving him, and because I had not placed his order, it would take at least twenty-five minutes for him to get his deep-fried hot dog on its stale fancy bun drowned in condiments which resembled body fluids. I was also embarrassed for him because he had elected to eat here, and if he wanted to meet the kind of men who ran along a river, he should not be eating from our menu, which would make him fat and farty and have stinky breath, and it was bad enough that he was wearing socks with sandals. He handed me back the dirty Wet One and not wanting to be collegial, I didn't take it. Hanging from his finger and stained green and gray, it wilted like a battered armistice flag, before it dropped to the ground. That Philly Dog won't make itself, I said, looking at the fryers.

Chicago Dog, he sighed.

Chicago Dog, I repeated, still with the ordering pad and pen in my hand. Beyond the food truck, sunlight chandeliered tree leaves and intensified the river's reedy smell. Wayne had finished eating and was watching a fly browse an open container of hot and sweet peppers. I thought about asking him to make the Chicago Dog so I could go out back and drain and then clean the fry oil containers before we moved to our night time location, but that would sound suspicious since no one ever wanted to do that particular side work chore because there were always a few cockroaches floating belly up in the oil, and Wayne was a nosy tattle-tale as it was.

Is that your boyfriend? Wayne asked.

No.

I saw the way you were talking to him. Wayne repeatedly slid the forefinger of one hand in and out of a circle he made with the forefinger and thumb on his other hand.

I took an all-beef hot dog out of a vat filled with finger-colored water and dumped it into a fryer. My ex-counselor walked over to a bench close to the scrub bearding the river and sat down. For six months, he had sat across from me for weekly one-on-ones and told me repeatedly that I was not a weak person, that I was, in fact (with the help of God's grace), a strong person, a person who had been forgiven, and because I didn't see the hand of God in my particular situation, I got my ex-counselor to talk instead. He told me that Jesus Christ had been his first true love, and that the sight of a man with wavy shoulder-length hair and a slim torso caused him much conflict and sometimes, when he was with his wife, he would picture Jeremy Sisto in *Jesus* in order to keep an erection, and when that stopped being effective, he knew it was time to get a divorce, so (with the assistance of Jim Caviezel in *The Passion of the Christ*) he cheated on his wife with a kindergarten teacher named Pam from their local parish so his wife would find out about it and leave him, and now when he had those moments of conflict, eating something deep-fried or exceptionally creamy was a way for him to calm down and regain grace. That's when he got up from his recliner chair and opened a desk drawer from which he grabbed a milk chocolate candy bar and handed it to me because there was much evil lurking in God's beautiful world, and conflict could come upon a person at any time.

Do you have a boyfriend? Wayne asked.

I squashed a mosquito lethargic with someone's blood before I pulled a potato bun out of a Styrofoam cooler and put it next to the toaster oven.

Ah, I get it. Wayne held two fingers in a V shape up to his mouth and licked between them.

A small group of teens had gathered at the menu board, so I went back to the ordering window. A girl in a white T-shirt over a Skittles-colored bra approached. Her light blue eyes had the startled quality of a deer caught in headlights. What's good?

I recommended the Boardwalk. I said, It's our best seller. I did not say, It's our best seller because it's mostly deep-fried potato drenched in salty malt vinegar. She ordered two Boardwalks, a Zing Dog, a Slaw Dog and a Bikini Dog, which I liked to make because I got to draw polka dots on the hot dog in cheese whiz. I dumped three more hot dogs into the meat fryer and two portions of tater tots into the vegan fryer and set about assembling their toppings instead of finishing my ex-counselor's order. I wanted him to wait because I wanted him to complain. I wanted him to ask God for strength as he threatened to tell The Manager I was a terrible Dog Wagoner so I could have a reason to hate this God-loving, self-deluding homosexual, a reason besides the fact that I had been weak, and I had needed him.

From the park bench, my ex-counselor caught my eye and pointed to his watch. I held up five fingers. He rested both hands on his thighs as if he had just received bad news. I imagined the buyer's remorse inside his head:

Good Lord, she's lost!

I should have gone to KFC.

The group of teens spread an old army blanket on the grass near the parking lot. There were three boys and two girls, and the boys were deciding how to divvy the girls up. The one who had ordered was the prize, being blond and blue-eyed and big-breasted, and two of the boys, alpha males in gym tanks and surfer shorts, were sharking around her. The other girl, Korean and knowledgeable about blond social capital, was vaping with the third boy, a carrot top drinking a beer. When the alpha males sandwiched the blond on the blanket, she doe-eyed her friend, who, acutely aware of her own un-blondness, made herself busy selecting music on her iPhone. In her testimony, Dr Ford recalled catching Mark Judge's eye, thinking he might help her when Brett Kavanaugh had his hand over her mouth and was trying to remove her clothes and she thought he might inadvertently kill her because she couldn't breathe, but Mark didn't help her, and no one helped me either, although when I was recovering in the Camp Geiger infirmary, I did receive some flowers with an anonymous note about friendly fire if I brought charges. I grabbed a bunch of napkins and some plastic forks and knives which had stuck together and walked over to the blanket.

Your food's ready. I cast a shadow over the threesome.

One of the alpha males looked up. Great.

You can pick it up.

Bring it to us. He muttered dipshit under his breath.

Brock, the blond scolded, She can hear you.

So?

From the iPhone, Ariana Grande sang about God being a woman, which was when my ex-counselor looked over and scowled. Where's my food?

It's coming.

Wayne was waiting for me at the ordering window. He thrust a cardboard tray containing a Chicago Dog at me, getting yellow mustard on my shirt.

Hurry up. It's getting cold. You don't want your boyfriend getting mad at you.

I walked back to my ex-counselor.

He took the tray from me. You've got something on your shirt.

Yeah.

He picked up his hot dog. It's cold.

I reached for his tray.

He yanked it away as his eyes fell on the alpha males.

God give me strength. Just leave it. Otherwise, I'll starve to death.

The blond had gone to the ordering window, where Wayne was trying to look down her shirt.

Hey, the alpha male who wasn't called Brock shouted. Hey! he repeated.

Yeah? I looked up from the mustard crusting my shirt.

Are you 21?

Yeah.

Would you get us some beer? You can keep the change. He waved a twenty at me.

No.

How about you Old Man?

My ex-counselor, still chewing, shook his head.

No joy, smirked the Korean girl. She stood up and tugged her shorts out of her ass. I'm taking a walk, she said to no one in particular and picked up her iPhone, shutting off Ariana Grande before she could finish singing about how she liked it.

Do you need anything else? I asked my ex-counselor.

Not right now.

I didn't tell him some shredded lettuce was stuck to his chin before I turned around and headed for the truck. On the way, I passed Wayne helping the blond carry her food back to the blanket. Carrot Top, Alpha Brock and Alpha Not-Brock were having a belching contest, which they asked Wayne to judge.

I decided to take a break. I put my ear buds back in and went around to the back of the truck. The back doors were a collage of waste. The Richmond Flying Squirrels mascots, Nutzy and Nutasha, smiled fiercely from giant holographic prism vending stickers, one on each door. Beneath them were fast food decals including a hot dog in a bun dancing in high top sneakers, a sun with a face made of tater tots, a monkey wearing sunglasses and a red flowered skirt holding a corndog up to its mouth and a penguin in a hipster hat drinking mountain fresh, bottled water. At the bottom was a peeling bumper sticker, its If You're Going To Ride My Ass, At Least Pull My Hair! slogan still legible. I sat on a fry oil container facing the access road and listened to Dr Ford apologize for not remembering how she got home on the night of her attack because she did not drive. The prosecutor drilled Dr Ford about the location of her house in relation to the vicinity where the attack had taken place and Dr Ford answered collegially while a Magnum ice cream bar wrapper danced around some cigarette butts and crushed soda cans littering the parking lot. Near its entrance, someone had run over an eastern cottontail rabbit, leaving it with its hind feet bent awkwardly under its flattened body. I didn't remember how I had gotten to the Camp Geiger infirmary after my attack but I knew I hadn't walked because before the rape my legs had been kicked out from under me and my back bruised. When some senator told Dr Ford that sharing her story would have a long-lasting impact on so many survivors, I laughed.

What's so funny, dipshit? Wayne was holding a half-eaten Zing Dog in one hand and the broken tip of a plastic knife in the other.

I removed my ear buds.

Recognize this? He thrust the knife tip forward. I had to comp them the hot dog. I'm telling my dad.

Sorry.

Get up front. Break time's over. Wayne opened the Nutzy door.

Get in. And your boyfriend wants to say goodbye.

Wayne didn't follow but shut the door behind me, probably so he could take a leak in private behind the truck. My ex-counselor was waiting for me at the ordering window. A watery booger threatened his left nostril. He took a toothpick from the Hot Diggity! dispenser and asked, Did you enroll in community college, meaning, Was I moving forward? I would never go back to school, having lost access to GI Bill benefits due to my dishonorable discharge for reporting my ex-commanding officer, and since my temperament was not suited to hot dog truck counter service, I would go on to fail at discount retail shop counter service, and then gas station counter service, making this my third to the last position dealing with the public; but I didn't know that yet and I said, No, but I'm going to next term when I've saved enough for tuition.

Good, he said, drumming his fingers on the counter in a way that made me think he had ordered something else. Then he added, The important thing is to have goals.

Wayne walked from behind the truck doing up his fly with one hand and carrying a to go bag in the other. When he saw my ex-counselor talking to me at the ordering window, he stopped behind him, planted his feet, and thrust his hips forward and back, over and over again, which made him look like he was twerking with a bad back. Then he joined his new friends on their blanket, squeezing in next to the Korean girl who had returned. From the to go bag, he took out several pieces of key lime cake, which the boys pounced on and the girls ignored.

In the streaky sunlight, the counter looked ashtray clean. I grabbed the least grimy rag from a hook adjacent to the fryers and wiped around my ex-counselor's elbow, hoping he might take the hint, but he didn't. He was busy watching the teens have a key lime cake fight on the army blanket. Then this man, my former counselor, began talking so philosophically about accountability and forgiveness that I felt an uncertain surprise.

The first time I met my ex-counselor was the day my sister drove me to the recovery program's halfway house. There was a balding wreath with a Welcome Home sign on the door and some plastic flowers in terracotta pots out front. Wood-carved twin dogs panted at the front door. East, west, home is best, my sister sing-songed as she led me across the faux wood foyer to a woman in a grey pantsuit eating something crunchy behind a reception desk. I sneered. Well, my sister said as she handed me my army duffel. Well, I replied. Okay then, she said, and was about to leave when my ex-counselor approached. Welcome to your new home, he said. My sister replied that I already had a home, and she didn't know what I was doing here because I wasn't crazy, I hadn't meant to kill myself, I had been raped, or so I claimed, and no one thought about how hard this was on her or the rest of The Family. Her voice became a little shrill. The few people who were in the living room, a woman with rose-colored hair and a man with James Franco lips, looked up from the daytime serial they were watching. My sister giggled nervously in their direction and said she was sure they weren't crazy either, and places like this were just a racket to get government money or turn a person against her family. When my ex-counselor suggested she calm down, she told him to calm down, that nothing fired a person up like being told to calm down and that as a counselor, she was surprised he didn't know that. She might have used words like "sham" and "cult" and "manipulative" before she told him to be quiet because she hadn't finished talking, but then it turned out she had because she didn't say anything else. My ex-counselor gave her his card in case she might want to talk, to which she giggled again and asked if he was hitting on her. He muttered God give me strength under his breath and then he assured her he wasn't, to which she asked why not and what did he think was wrong with her to give her his card in the first place.

During these pleasantries, I picked up my duffel and wandered into the living room, which smelled faintly of BO. The girl with the rose-colored hair was wearing a dress from that LA designer who made little girl clothes for grown up women. Were you really raped? she asked and then turned back to the TV. Later, she would share in group that she felt absolutely nothing, day in and day out, and that sometimes she heard the ringing of an old-fashioned cash register inside her head. James Franco Lips asked me if the woman screeching was my sister and then said we looked alike before he got up and went outside for a smoke. That's when my sister turned in my direction and asked if I was listening, to which I said yes, even though I wasn't, and she said good before reminding me that anger was a poison you mixed for a friend but drank yourself, and that she needed to get going because I knew how hard it was for her to drive in the dark with only one fully functioning eye, and she had her own life to attend to, and since I had gotten myself put into this place, the pressure was really on her to make The Family proud, and then she said, I'm going now, and turned around and left. My ex-counselor looked at the receptionist who had been eating Chips Ahoy cookies one after another and said, God helps us handle what we are given, before he looked at me and told me to bring my duffle back to reception so it and I could be searched, and then someone would show me to my room so I could unpack before our first session.

The session was held in a room full of futon sofas and throw blankets, bean bag chairs, and old maternity pillows. Everything was decorated in greens and yellows. I was sitting next to a middle-aged guy whose regular breathing was a constant, soft snore. My ex-counselor began by reminding us of The Golden Rule: honesty and no self-pity, which was really two rules, but I didn't say anything because I figured I wouldn't need to speak, but then he asked me to introduce myself, and when I still didn't say anything, he added, Whenever you're ready, but said it in a tone of voice that really says, "Now," so I said my name quickly, and added that I was addicted to Xanax and figured everyone had heard about everything else or soon would.

～

The cake fight turned into a wrestling match between Alpha Brock and Alpha Not-Brock. My ex-counselor turned to watch, as did a few other passersby trying to enjoy the tranquility of nature near a river's edge, and when he did, I finished wiping the counter, leaving greasy streaks across it.

Got anything creamy? he asked.

Churros. Chocolate or caramel?

I'll take the chocolate. He paid and went back to his bench as Not-Brock pinned Brock on the ground and Brock called, Uncle.

I dumped some churros into the vegan fryer and got a tin of chocolate sauce from a milk crate. A roach scrammed out from underneath it. Then, I hauled the hot plate out from its designated spot on the floor and plugged it in near the prep area. I poured chocolate sauce into a pan and put it on the hot plate, adding lots of extra cream. I wondered if my ex-counselor would ration out the chocolate sauce to the last churro or if he would use up all of the chocolate sauce on the first couple and not have any left for the remaining churros, which tasted like sugar-fried, oily cardboard if there was not chocolate or caramel sauce to mask that flavor, and how long it would take for him to need another food fix in order to calm down and regain grace.

It was after my ex-counselor gave me the milk chocolate bar that I began to talk in our one-on-one sessions. For one hundred and thirty-seven, sixty-minute meetings, my ex-counselor listened to me talk about student nursing aide training and Marine training, how to clean a rifle versus how to clean a bed pan, camaraderie and combat, why some people are believed while some people are not, the one or two things I wish I had done and one or two things I wished I hadn't, what makes an apology good or bad, and how sometimes the one person you need something from is the absolute one person you cannot ask, and how that need is a weakness.

The Korean girl jumped up and kicked Wayne hard in the nuts. She was about to kick him again but since she weighed maybe one hundred pounds, Alpha Not-Brock easily picked her up and moved her off the blanket, her feet still kicking the air.

What the fuck, Caitlin! he shouted, and I was surprised because she did not look like a Caitlin. You never kick a guy in the nuts, he said.

You do when he deserves it. That little shit tried to cop a feel, she fired back as she rained tiny punches on Alpha-Not-Brock's back and shoulders. Put me down, she demanded.

You liked it the first time, Wayne grimaced.

I thought the first time was an accident, the Korean girl yelled. I only let you sit next to me to be nice, because I felt sorry for you, you buck-tooth creep. But you can't be nice to creepers.

Wayne was trying hard not to cry but his face and neck got blotchy, so I could tell he wanted to. I took one of the churros from my ex-counselor's order and put it on an upturned plastic soda cup lid with a W drawn on it in chocolate sauce for Wayne to eat later. Then I assembled the remaining churros in a cardboard box top and sprinkled them with powdered sugar before I spooned the chocolate sauce into an extra-large dip container and delivered the whole thing to my ex-counselor with a flourish. His eyes got big as I set the chocolate sauce next to him on the pigeon poo splotched bench and handed him some napkins. The teens stood up and were gathering their things. Wayne got up too and limped past me saying I could take the rest of my break now. I followed Wayne to the truck to grab my ear buds and phone and continued in a wide arc farther down the river, where the air had hazed, rinsing the low bushes and weedy grass with grey film. A river otter glided out of the water, rubbed its slicked coat against the ground and then slid into its burrow. The defense had resumed questioning Dr Ford and when a female senator told Dr Ford she believed her, I cried a little.

My ex-counselor came up to me as Dr Ford was re-describing having to walk past her attackers to exit the house.

Sorry, I didn't mean to startle you, he said. He reached out and patted my arm. It was good to see you, he added. The thumb, index and ring fingernails on his right hand were outlined in chocolate sauce.

Good to see you too, I lied.

I'm going now, he said, but then he stood there and lingered for a moment as if to say, God, give her strength, but not so long as to say, God help you; it is obvious you are not whole; obviously you are still broken. My ex-counselor took a few steps before he bent down and picked something out of the gravel, which he tossed to me.

For luck, he said.

In my hand lay a penny.

Part 3

Oil lanterns threw soft shadows along the walls, and the women with their long flowing dresses and colored paper leis were dancing on a stage surrounded by wooden tables. We were sitting near the door at a table littered with beer bottles, overflowing ashtrays and bulb-shaped glasses of tea. Hoses from *shisha* pipes snaked between the men, Vera, and me. Vera was rolling a cigarette with an eye on the room, maybe because she sensed there was a story here, or maybe because that's how she had trained herself. I sat across from her, my neck grimy with muck and dust from the ISIS tunnels. Vera had brought me on an embed earlier. During an embed, a journalist followed a military unit into conflict so he could write something patriotic and cheery about the destruction of hospitals and schools and people, and then everyone could feel proud of his country as his president got a chance to flex his military muscle, and insurgents went on to fight another day.

Vera pulled her brassy blond hair into a sloppy ponytail, lit her rollie and leaned back in her chair. Like her, I kept one eye on the room but my other eye was on her. She was twenty-nine, pierced, and Russian, and over the last three years, she had been accompanying different rebel groups in Iraq and Syria to study how competing guerilla squads used labor market theory to get the best fighters. We met when Vera walked into the NGO where my ex-counselor had gotten me a God-given, last chance job, so she could run some money through the NGO's stateside bank account and avoid triple bank transfer fees. Lots of expats transferred money with the foreign NGOs, which needed the in-country cash flow to operate inside a war zone, so on the last Thursday of the month there would be a line of academics, researchers and consultants waiting with wads of new hundreds in the NGO's office, which was also the NGO staff apartment, to transfer money. On those nights, Heidi, the NGO's country director, would not sleep because she'd take the stacks of cash from the plastic bags taped to the underside of her sock drawer and play with them like building blocks on her bedroom floor.

Between tweets, Vera asked me what I was doing here, in northern Iraq, besides archiving photos for an organization which believed that Love Builds a Beautiful World, which she read off the corporate banner hanging above my desk in the living room, because I didn't look like someone who believed in the transformative power of love. I was curious to know how she had arrived at that conclusion but I didn't ask; instead I gave her the same spiel I had used in my interview when I said that after being in the military, I wanted to Make Love, Not Violence, which I had ripped off from the Core Values section on the About Us page of the NGO's website. Vera shook her head and pulled a rollie from behind her ear and was about to light it when my boss Heidi reminded her there was no smoking in the apartment, and then went into her bedroom to get the bill counting machine to count Vera's money. Vera joked that I should go on her next embed so I could see the making of violence just to know what I was up against, and then she gave the kind of laugh you give when you've inadvertently said something true.

I'll go, I said, I want to.

Her face went through a calculation of, If risk equals threat times vulnerability times impact, during which she looked me up and down and said, How long since you served? as if to say, Can you hack it? with a bit of, Is the adrenaline switched back on? because if the shit hits the fan, everyone will need to fight, and I said, About fifteen months, to mean Pain is acceptable, and Yes, I can do great and terrible things because the marines taught me how to.

The following Sunday was the start of #MyActionsMatter, an international feel-good fest to raise awareness of violence against women. For sixteen days, foreign dignitaries, NGO communications officers, UNHCR, UNAMI and other alphabet soup advisors would arrive to give speeches and take photos in the High Ministry offices with local government bigwigs and then retire to their hotels in the Christian city of Ainkawa, where alcohol was served in bars and clubs and restaurants, and there were brothels on almost every Christian corner. During the opening ceremony, the prime minister of the region would give a speech where he promised to show "full leniency" towards women to achieve gender equality before going home to both his wives. On the second to the last night of the campaign, a local taxi driver would pick up a fare on her way to her Ainkawa hotel room after a Woman4Woman Campaign gala dinner and take her instead to an empty lot in a deserted area where he would assault her and leave her before returning home in time for 'Isha prayer. When the security police arrested the driver, emoji reactions on the local news' Facebook page ranged from Angry, as if to say, He did nothing wrong. How dare he be arrested? Everyone knows western women ask for it, and, What was she wearing?, or Sad, to say, That's too bad, but praise Allah it wasn't one of our good Muslim women, or LOL, from those responders who understood irony. Those were the locals who worked with gender protection organizations and received death threats, who were not surprised when the taxi driver eventually got off, who knew how hollow any government initiative, lenient or not, was bound to be.

Heidi came back into the living room, carrying the bill counting machine in the folds of her embroidered muumuu. She was thin and middle-aged and dressed like Mrs. Roper to conceal her big boobs, which she thought showed respect for the local culture. Oh, go where? I want to come.

Vera took in the rows of potted micro greens thriving in the afternoon sunlight, the homemade mats made from plastic bags beneath them, and the worm terrarium beside the office printer. An embed with the *Pesh Merga*, Vera answered. You wouldn't like it, she added.

Heidi didn't like being told what she liked. She shoved Vera's wad of bills into the counting machine as Vera told me where and when to meet, which meant Vera had to repeat herself when the machine stopped counting. Heidi then told her that we had a lot of work to do and that she appreciated her stopping by, but now it was time to go and maybe she should think about wearing a cardigan or some kind of shirt over her tank top the next time she wanted to launder her money because anyone could see her walk into our office dressed *like that* and people here judged you by the company you kept, and she had a certain image to maintain as the local face of the NGO. Vera and I both sneered a little, and I knew then that I would go with her.

Heidi would get mad that I chose the embed over her Thanksgiving potluck, which she always held for a select group of American expats but not for her non-American co-workers and friends because Thanksgiving was "for Americans," and how did it look that her own roommate and subordinate didn't attend her potluck, especially since she had assigned me the responsibility of peeling, cooking and mashing potatoes for twenty people. When both I and the potatoes were no shows, which meant there was no vegetarian side dish with which to make gravy boats, Heidi would curse me in her outdoor voice for ruining her Thanksgiving and blare some Christian heavy metal rock music while she drank counterfeit sherry and directed dish duty. This would result in a noise complaint made to the building's management office from two young women who worked for a rival NGO in the apartment above ours, whom Heidi often policed for what they were wearing. When Heidi received the official notice of complaint, she would blame me for being selfish and disloyal and irresponsible, and tell me I was incapable of demonstrating any kind of love, let alone the kind of love big enough to unmake violence, which would make that day the last day I stayed in her apartment.

But this day had been different. Our group was an informal mix of part-time, taxi-driving *Pesh Merga* soldiers and two freedom fighters, a Glaswegian named Iain and a Texas Ranger wannabe named Christopher, both of whom had come on their own to fight ISIS. Because Iain and Christopher had over-stayed their visas and did not have the thousands of dollars needed to pay their accruing fines, they were hiding out with a Canadian oil entrepreneur and his wife in a house in Ainkawa as they waited for the oil entrepreneur to grease some strings and get their visas backdated and their fines forgiven. Together, our ragtag band of brethren took two taxis through multiple checkpoints where other *Pesh Merga* guards recognized our drivers and waved us through without inspection all the way to Mosul.

Most of the old city was pulverized, as if some giant had had a temper tantrum across every block and broken all the marble, and now all that was left on either side of the streets were mounds of dirt and rubble. As we drove, Vera pointed out various locations bombed by the US in support of the Iraqi security forces and then asked what I was going to do to unmake that violence. I said I was going to use the love that builds a beautiful world to put a Walmart *there*, and a Starbucks *there*, and a mega mall with a cineplex, indoor swimming pool and fast food court *there* across the street and connect them with a skywalk. Vera responded it was a little too late for love as those who were left in the city did not look kindly upon Americans, so I should not speak outside the car, and then she handed me a headscarf from her backpack as our driver pulled over near a mountain of debris on the eastern outskirts of town. In the detritus were unexploded ammunition, cooking pots, Kevlar vests, and flowered blankets. A child's hand silted with dirt lay near a home-made rag doll, the heart sewn onto its chest partially burned off. The other taxi pulled up behind us, the driver's prayer beads swinging from the rearview mirror.

Vera introduced our *Pesh Merga* driver as Sardar and the other taxi's *Pesh Merga* driver as Sarbast. Both were medium and mustached and wore shirts with buttons straining over their bellies. We had a round of introductions, which were not strictly necessary since we did not share a common language and no one but Vera would probably see them after today. With the *Pesh Merga* soldiers in the lead, we walked through the outlying villages towards an ancient monastery, my marine instincts kicking in. Both Iain and Christopher began to stink like vinegar. Iain was short and compact and hated Putin but wanted to fuck Vera, who towered over him by at least 8 inches. He'd ask her to go dancing at one of the Ainkawa hotel bars and she'd say, Sure, and he'd say, I'll call you, but everyone knew he wouldn't. Christopher was medium and slight and saw himself as a lone wolf, ready to die heroically in some righteous battle of good versus evil because God had told him to come here. He liked to hock snot onto the tan-colored sand. The *Pesh Merga* ignored everyone but Vera because she was paying them and because they thought she was CIA, which they asked me about using charades.

The inside of the monastery was crowded with sacks of dirt and rubble, its relics long ago looted and sold on the black market by ISIS. There was a large uneven square the size of a kitchen table cut into the chapel floor and reinforced with metal railings. On one side of it, a wooden ladder hung straight down, flush against a jagged earthen wall. At the bottom, there were more sacks of dirt, a jerry can for fuel and a generator. Two steps had been carved into the floor to mark the beginning of a tunnel which descended steeply for several meters before levelling off, its sides bearing the strike marks of pick axes. Extension cords ran along the tunnel ceiling, which was supported by wooden beams, to power the lanterns and naked light bulbs hanging overhead. Every two meters, one side of the tunnel would widen into a semi-circle shaped alcove. Some of these alcoves contained plastic bags of snacks, usually sesame seed cookies. The *Pesh Merga* explained in Kurdish to Vera, who translated, that the alcoves relieved underground traffic jams as ISIS fighters ran from one location to another in surprise attacks on the Iraqi military or the *Pesh Merga* forces. When Sarbast mimed striking the ground with the butt of his Kalashnikov and then turning very quickly and striking another spot, Vera nodded her head and said Wack-a-Mole, which he repeated several times because he found it fun to say, I think.

Farther in, thin mattresses were propped up sideways against the walls under graffiti that proclaimed Victory is the Battle of the Islamic State and There is no God but Allah. In a makeshift cubicle fashioned from sheets of plastic and wooden beams, there was a kitchen, recently vacated. Plastic gallon jugs of water lined the wall next to a cheap table where a hot plate and a pot of coagulating chickpeas sat. Above the hot plate, there was a cooking roster that listed what the fighters' daily menu was, but nothing on the list matched the contents of the kitchen, which contained bags of dates, an open jar of honey, an uncorked bottle of cooking oil and a brown plastic milk crate full of eggs, some of which had cracked, yellow yolk dribbling down their sides. I thought about the Core Values posters touting honor, courage and commitment hanging in the mess hall at Camp Geiger as I watched a rat run out from under an old Ramadan calendar lying on the floor. Iain cursed, Ya, wee small cunt! and kicked a half-rolled up tube of Relief gel after it. Christopher reminded him that there were ladies present and then apologized for Iain's cunting, to which Vera replied that it was okay, that everybody should feel free to cunt away, but could Christopher please move so she could film what was left of some medical equipment and bandages, many of which were damp and bloodied, on her iPhone.

Past the kitchen, the tunnel shrank, but Vera was the only one who had to really stoop to go through it. Walking over a cardboard box for a flat screen TV, we arrived at a room kitted out with a doubled mattress, blankets, towels, and cheap, flowered wall paper. A few ISIS posters had been taped up and Koranic verses had been written onto the blades of a portable fan in red marker. On the floor, Christopher found a piece of paper outlining the rules of how to pray on Fridays, how to pray when you travel and how to pray before battle, which he palmed into his pocket, not that anyone cared. One of the *Pesh Merga*, it might have been Sardar, explained this was the sleeping room of an *emir*, who, due to his higher rank, was afforded a few luxuries. I snickered at a mirror hanging above a shelf containing a comb, a bottle of cologne and the Koran. My ex-commanding officer was always well-groomed, looking GI Joe action figure perfect, even when he booted me to the floor and tore me. When Christopher reached for the Koran, Sardar leveled his Kalashnikov, ready to shoot him. Christopher screamed, What the fuck rag head! after he heard a round feeding into the chamber. He put his hands up as Iain pulled out a Glock 17, which made Sarbast level his Kalashnikov at Iain and disengage its safety and then shout something important-sounding to Vera. Before I left that morning, I had taken one of Heidi's kitchen knives and tucked it inside one of my combat boots, but for now I kept it where it was. This was the best time I'd had since my dishonorable discharge. Vera shouted at Christopher to get away from the Koran because it had been booby trapped with an IED, there was a firing button on the side, and for Iain to lower his weapon for fuck's sake unless he wanted to get us all killed. Christopher's Adam's apple bounced down and up exactly once before he took a slow step backwards, hands still in the air. Because Sardar was directly behind him with his Kalashnikov still pointed at Christopher's back, Sardar had to step backwards too, which they did in tandem, which reminded me of Kabuki theater. Then, Vera said something in Kurdish, which made both *Pesh Merga* lower their Kalashnikovs, Iain lower his Glock and Christopher finally lower his hands after he wiped his eyes.

The tunnel narrowed again and sloped steeply upward. Rough, tall steps had been hewn into the floor so that climbing them was like scaling the side of a mountain. Near the surface, the air became warmer as sunlight smeared through openings hacked into the tunnel's ceiling, which allowed for additional airflow and served as lookout points or sniper positions. Stepping over crumbled water bottles, pieces of twine, Turkish snack cake wrappers and a sheer pink scarf, we climbed out of the tunnel onto the side of a small hill about 200 meters from the monastery, the exit partially obscured by rocks, and dirt-covered pieces of wood. I would wonder about that scarf, to whom it had belonged, if she had come willingly to the tunnel or if she had been taken by force, perhaps bought at an ISIS sex slave market, or made a recent widow of *jihadi* war, if she had been excited or scared, or excited and then scared, or if any part of her wished she had never made it out of the tunnel alive, assuming she had.

Tan, sandy dirt stretched down from the hill toward the horizon. The *Pesh Merga* warned us to walk in their footsteps because sometimes the areas around an entrance were booby-trapped. We made our way slowly, carefully stepping around rocks and small weeds, eyes on the pebbly ground, which is where Vera spotted it, and which is why she later referred to this discovery as hitting pay dirt. Trampled flat and covered with boot prints was a small messenger bag containing soft notebooks and hard USB sticks. Many, but not all, of the sticks had been broken. Those that were not, as well as the notebooks, contained proficiency ratings for fighters from multiple ISIS cells and *jihadi* franchises such as AQAP, al-Nusra Front, and Ahrar al-Sham, much like player stats on baseball cards. The fighters were ranked according to their adherence to religious and behavioral codes, military achievements including kills and the number of battles fought, level of discipline, capacity to build trust, mental agility and specialized expertise. There was a separate column for notes describing what might lure certain fighters away from their present group. This discovery would further Vera's research, which would later be published in *Foreign Policy* and cited by the Kellogg School of Management, Harvard's Kennedy School of Economics and the Pentagon, among others, and in the lead up to the 2020 elections would cement her seat on the Sunday morning talk show circus as President Trump brought the country to the brink of war.

We hiked back to the taxis in high spirits. The *Pesh Merga* wanted to take us somewhere special to celebrate Vera's find and us not getting ourselves blown up, a place different from the places foreigners usually went to, a place that I, in particular, might enjoy. Vera shrugged her shoulders at me when she translated this. Iain and Christopher were game, not having anything better to do than sit around the Canadian oil entrepreneur's house, drinking and smoking and telling stories about Iain's hairy buttocks, and I wanted to run the clock out on Heidi's Thanksgiving Extravaganza. Piling into the taxis, we reached the outskirts of Ainkawa long after dark. I was surprised the *Pesh Merga* didn't drive into Ainkawa, where most nightlife was located, but kept going until we reached a large white-walled building with a domed, corrugated tin roof shaped like bat wings and a huge Tuborg beer sign above the entrance, across the highway from Family Mall. All eyes were on us as we walked in, maybe because Iain and Christopher were singing old Calvary songs or maybe because Vera and I were women. Iain liked the rock star status, peacocking his way over to the gun check to drop his Glock liked he owned the place whereas Christopher strutted through like a Christmas elf learning how to walk with a stick up its ass.

Drinks appeared, although we had not ordered, beers for the Western-ers and tea for the *Pesh Merga*, along with two *shisha* pipes, to which Sardar and Sarbast attached yellow plastic mouth pieces. When I took out some money to pay for the round, Sardar elbowed Sarbast, gestured to the stage and laughed. I looked at Vera, who was busy reading emails on her phone and then to Iain and Christopher, who were having a chugging contest. Christopher was performing his famed party trick where he held the bottle in his mouth with his teeth and no hands and tipped his head back to swal-low, but Iain won. I offered two twenty-five thousand Iraqi dinar notes to the *Pesh Merga*, which was about forty dollars and was equal to one tenth of the monthly income full-time *Pesh Merga* earned for risking their lives to fight ISIS. I didn't know how much the adjuncts made. The twenty-five thousand Iraqi dinar bills were red and crisper and newer than the green ten thousand Iraqi dinar notes, which were still in pretty good condition as compared to the dark blue five thousand Iraqi dinar notes, which were worn and permanently wrinkled, but not so much as the tan-colored one thousand Iraqi dinar notes, which were often held together by tape but were not as shabby as the lighter blue two hundred and fifty Iraqi dinar notes, which looked like they had been through a washing machine more than a few times, their edges so tattered the bills were no longer rectangular. Sardar took the money and pointed at the stage and then at me and then again to the stage, where the lights had dimmed, and women in long flowing dresses and colored-paper leis had glided on and begun to sway.

I shrugged my shoulders.

He said something that sounded like "Zherwanna" and pointed again at the dancing women. Beautiful, no? he asked.

Yes, I said, but I didn't mean it.

You? he held up my two red Iraqi dinar notes and gestured to an imaginary necklace around his neck before he pointed again to a group of dancers at the far end of the stage.

I shrugged my shoulders.

He gestured again to his imaginary necklace and then pointed at a cluster of old and ugly dancing women wearing tan-colored leis, mismatched foundation streaking down their necks. He asked did I wanna fuck, which was something Sardar knew how to say.

I turned to Vera.

Sardar said something to Vera, which made her laugh. Vera then explained that Sardar thought I was giving him money to purchase one of the dancers for the night, and for fifty thousand Iraqi dinars, I could choose from the women in the tan-colored leis. I looked again at the dancers on the stage, their eyes vacant beneath masks of makeup. The leis were not leis but necklaces of Iraqi dinars. A girl of about ten was wearing a brown necklace made of many, many 50,000 Iraqi dinar bills.

I was trying to pay for the round, I said.

We'll pay at the end. Vera lit a rollie.

That girl should be in bed, I said pointing at the ten-year-old.

She will be soon enough.

That's not what I meant. I stood up from the table.

Where are you going? Vera picked a piece of loose tobacco from her tongue.

Bathroom.

I'm not sure there's a woman's WC here. This kind of place is usually men only. Better take one of the guys with you. Vera gestured to Christopher and Iain, who were standing with a man at the corner of the stage. Christopher was watching Iain, and Iain was pointing at a dancer wearing a green-colored lei. After some negotiation, Iain handed the man a wad of cash and the man beckoned to the dancer and then led Iain and Christopher up a flight of stairs. I was half-expecting Christopher to immediately return, leading the girl by her wrist, having bought her outright just so he could play the hero and smuggle her far away to save her. He'd take her to his piss-ant Texan hometown and force her to learn English so she could read the Bible. This, of course, did not happen, probably because Christopher was a bit cheap, which is why Iain had paid for the dancer in the first place. He'd offered to share his session maybe because he liked an audience, or maybe because he felt a little sorry for Christopher and was a generous guy. As I made my way outside, I guessed at how their pre two-on-one conversation would go:

Ya cannae be touching my arsehole when I'm gettin' it on with the wee slag.

I'm not a faggot, you fucking Ned.

Nae doubt you'll watch.

I'll go first and you can watch.

Yer off yer heid. I paid. I'm goin' furst.

~

Outside the air was cool. I walked around the building, away from the harsh red glare of the Family Mall sign. At the back of the building, I stood in some weeds listening to the swoosh of cars speeding along the highway before I pulled down my pants and squatted to pee. At that moment, I was just a person peeing in a field and in the next, I was a person peeing on my shoes as a drunk and bearded laughing man approached me. The green-black field dissolved into the brown-paneled walls of my ex-commanding officer's office, and there was the ghost echo of a .45 being locked and loaded against the base of my skull, my ex-commanding officer's clean-shaven face inches from my own. This was not a time to be collegial. Reaching into my boot, I grabbed Heidi's kitchen knife and drove it into the bearded man's groin and pulled it out as his dirt- colored pants darkened. He stumbled and I stumbled, him because he was drunk and wounded, me because my pants were still around my ankles. He swung at me and missed. I swung at him, knife in hand, and connected. He fell down and I stood up, pulling my pants with me and trucked around the bat-shaped building to the highway and continued running before I realized the knife was still in my hand. I bent down and cleaned it in the overgrown grass and put it back inside my boot and took stock of where I was. I needed to go back to the table so as not to arouse suspicion and I needed to get as far away from the table as possible. I slowed my breathing and walked back toward the Tuborg sign above the entrance but then passed it, around the side of the building to the back, where I paused and breathed, and looked and listened but did not investigate, before I returned to the entrance and walked inside.

Plates of sliced green apples and quartered oranges had been set on the table. Christopher was sitting there, nursing a beer, his nose bloodied and his eyes beginning to swell. Vera was reading one of the notebooks she had found. Iain was nowhere in sight.

What happened to you? I nodded at Christopher.

What happened to you? Vera looked up from her notebook to my hands, which were grimed, my fingertips a little bloody.

I had to pee, I said, And I got my period. I took a few Kleenex from the box on the table and wiped my fingers. My right shirt cuff was also a little stained, so I folded it under to hide it.

Gross. Christopher moved the plate beyond my reach. Don't touch the fruit.

I shoved the used tissues into my pocket. I won't, I said, and then, I think I'm going to go.

Vera packed up the notebook, I'll come with you. Sardar can bring us now and Sarbast can take Christopher and Iain when Iain's finished.

Christopher stood. I'll go now too.

Vera said something to the *Pesh Merga* and Sardar stood from the table. He would drive us to our respective homes where, after I eventually got into the apartment, I would take the knife from my boot and wash it and put it back in the utensil drawer, where Heidi would find it and use it to chop tomatoes and peppers for her tofu stir-fry as she gave me the silent treatment.

In the flickering light of the oil lanterns, the dancers spinning in their watercolor dresses looked almost elegant, so you could almost forget about the violence that had brought them there. Sarbast was happily sucking on his *shisha* pipe, swaying his head gently to the rhythm of the dancers' hips like most of the men in the room were, and I wondered about his wife, and about the wives of all the men swaying their heads, and then about the dancers, if they were or had been wives, if they had ever had sex for their own pleasure or as an expression of love, if they believed, or had ever believed in love, and if even one of them thought love could unmake violence.

Part 4

The Kurdish flag rippled in the light breeze. The wooden dinghy with its outboard motor was ferrying people, food, and medical supplies across the blue-brown water. Behind us, the grassy embankment with its thin trees grew smaller as we puttered across the Tigris River toward the empty, silty dirt of Syria. Leila, a Jordanian working for an Italian NGO, pulled the black and white *kaffiyeh* around her neck up over her nose as she side-eyed me, maybe because she was wondering how I was faring or maybe because she was second guessing her choice to bring me. My breath stank, my eyes were bloodshot and what I owned lay in the duffel bag at my feet. We had been traveling all day, first to document a cholera outbreak at the Domiz refugee camp, where we counted water stations and mapped latrines before sitting down as honored guests for a camp lunch, and then to pick up supplies in Dohuk, where the Italian NGO's head office was located. Because the Syrian government did not want its Kurdish population to gain independence, many of the NGOs serving Syrian Kurds set up in northern Iraq and sent their aid workers overland via Turkey, where the taxi drivers made you smuggle cartons of cigarettes in your suitcases as part of the fare to Syria, or you were sent over water via expat privilege, enjoying priority boarding on tiny boats while the locals who needed to flee waited on the riverbank to cross into the Rojava region of Syria, where the Kurdish self-rule movement was strongest. Leila worked on women's empowerment issues, and her NGO had to be careful it didn't inadvertently train female soldiers for the YPJ when it was training the women of Rojava in self-defense. The YPJ was the sister arm of the YPG, which Turkey considered a militia arm of the PPK, which was considered a terrorist group by the USA and Turkey. This didn't stop the US from arming and training the YPG to fight the last remnants of ISIS in Syria, nor did it stop Turkey from shelling the YPG in Syria as the YPG fought ISIS even though Turkey and the US were fighting on the same side, but it did stop the YPG's ISIS offensive, so in the end there was a lot of fighting and dying in Rojava, but not by ISIS.

I was watching as our boat approached the people on the Syrian side of the river, their trash bags of belongings growing bigger as we got closer. Like me, the people at the river's edge were also watching our boat approach, anxious for their turn to board it and motor back across the narrow river to safety. The motor sputtered off and the boat drifted onto the brown riverbank, where the waiting people immediately swarmed it. The man steering the boat beat them back with a metal pole as the passengers unloaded their humanitarian aid. Leila and I swung plastic bags full of bandages, gauze, sanitary napkins, hydrogen peroxide, ibuprofen, and amoxicillin onto the damp ground aiming for a man whose big hair made him look like a hitman from *The Sopranos*. Leila swore as a plastic bag containing clean blankets tore open and spilled onto the muddy bank. She was petite and efficient and had taken pity on me when she found me curled up under my jacket in the hallway outside my apartment door the night of the embed because Heidi had locked me out. Leila lived with Giulia in the apartment above ours, and when the electricity cut out and they had to take the stairs, they found me. I was shaking and smelled vaguely of pee. Pausing to catch her breath on the landing, Giulia was flipping off Heidi's hand-painted acorn wreath hanging on the apartment door when Leila spotted me. After I told them that I had been locked out, Giulia had some things to say about Americans in general and some more things to say about know-it-all, proselytizing, stick-a-knife-in-your-back do-gooders in particular before Leila invited me to sleep in their apartment for the night. There might have been other words on Giulia's part such as "petty" and "control freak" and "hypocritical" when my egregious deed of missing the potluck was divulged. These were words we all liked. Giulia used more words when she fired a frothy email to the building's management office while I was in the shower. By the end of the next day, I would once again be in Leila and Giulia's apartment but this time with my packed duffle and an invitation to volunteer with an NGO, whose overall mission was to prevent new conflicts in the Middle East, which, in this case, included Heidi's apartment.

Grabbing my duffel, I followed Leila off the boat to an open-bed truck where our supplies were already being loaded by the big-haired man, who was polite in a challenging way. Leila introduced him to me as our driver, Hama, and then switched into Arabic as she lit a cigarette and continued talking to him. As I headed back to the riverbank for our supplies, I imagined their smoke-break conversation:

New volunteer?

Yes.

Disaster tourist?

I don't think so.

A total disaster?

Probably. Who else would work here for free?

I rested the muddy blankets on the bumper of the truck and opened some of the supply bags. I was combining their contents so I could free up a bag to put the blankets in, and also to see if there was any Xanax, when the blankets fell on the ground. Finishing her cigarette, Leila came around the back of the truck to see what I was doing.

You're stepping all over the blankets.

Sorry, I said as I picked them up and stuffed them into a now empty bag.

Where did you get that bag?

I merged the stuff from the bags that weren't full.

Leila swore under her breath. The supplies aren't going to the same place. They're packed by destination because we've got two drops and the two places don't get the same things.

Sorry, I said, and this time I was.

It's okay, Lelia took the bag from my hands, Your jacket's wet. You should get in the truck.

This is the last of it, Hama said as he approached us. Even with his arms full, he walked like a hitman.

Good. Put it there. Leila pointed to a corner of the truck bed as she reorganized the mess I had made. I walked to passenger side of the truck and climbed into the backseat as Hama got behind the wheel. He watched me with bug eyes from the rearview mirror until Leila got into the truck, and we drove away.

It was dark by the time Hama stopped the truck in front of a metal rail gate painted white, the words J-I-N and W-A-R mounted atop either side of it. The closed gate blocked the dirt road, which was flanked by wheat fields. Into the glow of the truck's headlights walked a woman, a Kalashnikov slung over her shoulder. Another woman, also holding a rifle, looked out from a mud brick guard house just inside the gate, to the right. As the guard approached the driver's side window, she smiled in recognition at Hama and Leila before she swept a mirror around the underside of the truck and then nodded at the other guard who spoke into a walkie talkie and the gate doors swung open. Hama drove through and parked beyond the guard house. In the distance, the headlights illuminated a semi-circle of mud brick, one-story buildings. A woman carrying a basket exited one of the buildings and walked towards us.

That day had been the official opening of Jinwar, a women-only, ecological self- sustaining village started two years ago and built from scratch by Syrian Kurdish women. On a plot of stony dry land, they planted trees, seeded gardens, made mud bricks and built buildings to create a place for women who wanted to live independently and break free from violence. Officially, I had been brought here to teach the women of Jinwar self- defense in case ISIS attacked them like it had the Yazidis at Sinjar, but ISIS mostly left Jinwar alone because their fighters believed if they were killed by a woman, they would not go to paradise and collect their forty virgins. The real threat came from the surrounding community, where not everyone believed that women should live freely. For the next five weeks, in the Women's Academy building, where the principles of *Jineoloji* were taught under a banner which read "Without Women There Is No Freedom," I would show sixteen women and some of the commune's thirty-two children how to shout in someone's face, push back, leverage body weight and use knees, elbows and heads to channel fear into survival. We practiced kneeing groins, gouging eyes and elbowing noses if someone approached you but didn't practice what to do if someone kicked you to the ground and held a .45 to the base of your skull and pulled your pants down and ripped into you because no amount of kneeing and gouging and elbowing could defend against that unless you had a .45 too, and the only guns allowed in Jinwar were the rusty Kalashnikovs the guards had at the front gate. Instead, I explained how to maximize damage on an assailant by having an everyday object such as a pen or keys or sand or dirt in your hand if, say, you were approached in an isolated place alone at night but I didn't talk about what might happen if your everyday ordinary object was a knife, or how you might feel about using that knife after you had. I didn't have an explanation for that, yet, except that I thought Gandhi was wrong because an eye for an eye didn't leave the world blind so much as it left part of the world regretting something it had done while the other part of the world went on doing what it always did, sans regrets, and not doing something when someone took your eye or your virginity without asking was no picnic either.

The academy was located between the Asnan Bakery and My Sister's Shop, a store of handicraft items made in the commune that would have made Heidi screech, They're so cute! They're so cute! as she dug her fingernails into their embroidered stitches or picked at their beads and glue. The academy also housed the Jinwar Council, whose leadership rotated every month but was now being run by Fatma, who was the woman carrying the basket, Leila explained, as Fatma reached the truck. Hama, Leila, and I got out of the truck and stood like members of a wedding party waiting to receive the guests. Hama put his hand over his heart to greet Fatma, who mirrored his gesture before kissing Leila on both cheeks and then handing her the basket which was filled with peppers, eggplants, tomatoes and cucumbers. Leila protested exactly three times before accepting it and then introduced me to Fatma as Jinwar's newest volunteer. I put my hand over my heart and bowed a little, which made Fatma laugh because she said she wasn't used to people bowing to her but she liked it, and she could see herself getting used to it, and was this what it was like for men, Hama? and no wonder they did everything they could to control women and maintain patriarchy. We all laughed except for Hama, who understood some English but not a lot, and in response took Fatma's basket of vegetables to the bed of the truck and returned with the supplies we had brought for the commune and my duffle. As we walked towards Sifajin Natural Health Center with our bags of penicillin and hydrogen peroxide, Leila asked Fatma how the opening had gone and Fatma said really well, some reporters had come, what with the opening falling on The International Day for the Elimination of Violence Against Women, and everyone was so surprised that women from different backgrounds could get along well enough to build something, let alone a self-sustaining village, but the biggest surprise was when the Jinwar women sat down to eat when the male visitors did and not after, as was customary. This had caused a disturbance because some people who were men thought that other people who were women should wait to eat until the men had had their fill in case there wasn't enough food, which there was, because it turned out that women were pretty good at growing things too, which is why Fatma was able to give Leila a big basket of vegetables. Then Fatma pointed out the communal kitchen table in the courtyard and explained that's where some shouting had taken place when the women sat down to eat with the men, and the words *haram a'aleik*, which meant "shame on you," had been used, probably with regard to more than eating at the same time. Fatma then turned to me and explained that I was expected to take my turn doing the cooking because bonds were made through bread and sweat, and that I'd be staying at her house with her six daughters, who were very excited to meet me. I sneered a little but figured it was dark enough so nobody could see.

Inside the health center was bright and white. On a wall opposite a row of plastic chairs was the decorative highlight, a mural of a giant white five-petal flower with a cluster of yellow-green stamens pushing up from its center. We deposited our goody bags on the corner of a homemade wooden table and unpacked them. Fatma didn't want the pills or the peroxide, but Leila insisted, saying winter was coming and although alternative medicine was useful, there was no harm in accepting some help from modern science, especially when it came to bacterial infections or disinfecting the children's cuts and scrapes, and that the health center didn't have to use it if it really didn't want to, but wasn't it better to have it on hand just in case? Fatma jerked her head in my direction, saying modern science didn't seem to be doing me any favors, so thanks but no thanks all the same. She was more conflicted about accepting the sanitary pads, unsure of whether their convenience offset their negative ecology factor, but was grateful for the bandages and gauze. I repacked the hydrogen peroxide, penicillin and ibuprofen into a plastic bag and handed it to Hama, who gave it to Leila, who put it back down on the table. We should go, Leila said to Hama, It's getting late, she explained to Fatma and embraced her, calling, Good luck, to me over Fatma's shoulder.

After Hama and Leila left, Fatma threw the amoxicillin into a trash can and took the rest of the booty into the adjacent room, which I assumed to be the examining room although I did not follow her because without the lure of Xanax, I didn't really like rooms in hospitals anymore. When she came out, I was staring at the five-petal flower. She told me the flower was called *Peganun Harmala* or Syrian Rue and that it was the symbol for Jinwar, which meant women's space, because depending on how the seeds, petals, or leaves were used, Syrian Rue could cure over 200 illnesses and remove negative thoughts, much like how women could accomplish many, many things when they were given the freedom to use all their abilities and talents. I figured this symbolism to be a stretch, especially if you needed to explain it, and, instead of being understood as an I-told-you-so to the world, could be seen as just an ordinary flower. Then she told me she'd brew me some Syrian Rue tea when we got to her house and that I should drink it every day while I was there to cure me of whatever negativity was plaguing me. I thought it would take a lot more than flower tea to de-plague me but I didn't say so. Instead, I asked her if she had served the tea at today's opening festivities and she said yes, of course, and how did I think she got all those indignant men to stop shouting?

I entered the Women's Academy after breakfast the next morning. Like the waiting room at the health center, the classroom was also painted white and had a mud brick floor. A large mural of a half-woman, half-serpent dominated the main wall. Fatma explained that the figure was Shahmaran, Queen of the Serpents, who was all-knowing and beautiful, and whose creation myth centered on not judging others because looks could be deceiving. I thought about my ex-commanding officer's GI Joe action figure face and then I thought about the bearded drunk man laughing in the field. Then I thought about what my ex-commanding officer did and what I didn't do, and then I thought about what the man in the field didn't do and what I did do, and then I excused myself and took a quick walk in the communal garden to cry a little in the watermelon patch. When I came back, some women had assembled, so I apologized for being late and then we spent the next thirty minutes shouting Back Off! in each other's faces before we pushed each other's chests *hard* in order to get away. Some of the women sounded like mice when they shouted, and I felt sorry for them because I knew that my short stint of training would not reverse a lifetime of being programmed to be collegial. Others had faces of fury, corking a built-up rage desperate to be released. I had a hard time looking at those women because I knew no amount of self-defense training could unmake the violence they had already experienced. The best they could hope for was to be better prepared the next time, because there always seemed to be a next time. After the session, Fatma passed around cups of her Syrian Rue tea, which we all drank, and which I later learned contained a powerful anti-depressant and was a hallucinogen but was not addictive, and then I followed the other women into the courtyard and looked for a way to be truly useful.

I found it in the open-air communal kitchen. On the tiled kitchen floor beneath a mural of a woman wearing a blue dress and holding a leafed tree in one hand and a leafless tree in the other, I sat with two older women dicing vegetables from the communal garden in preparation for lunch. They smiled semi-toothed grins and handed me a knife and a plastic Tupperware container with the lid securely fastened so I could use it a chopping board and then nodded at the pile of tomatoes and cucumbers on a round tin platter. The knife was similar to but not quite the same as Heidi's kitchen knife. I sliced into a tomato, which bled its juice and seeds, and wondered who was prepping the free condiments for the Hot Diggety! condiments dispenser at The Dog Wagon.

A woman came into the kitchen for some cold water and it took me a minute to recognize her as the guard with the Kalashnikov from the night before because she looked smaller without a rifle strapped to her shoulder. She nodded at me and then stooped to kiss the cheeks of each woman chopping vegetables before she filled her water container and went back outside, past a cluster of women tilling soil with their bare hands, a group of women making mud bricks, and another pulling weeds in the garden, to the playground area where she picked up a hammer and resumed building a jungle gym. Occasionally, a child's shriek would break the ker-thunk of our knives hitting our makeshift chopping boards. While we were chopping, one of the women began singing to herself, eyes on her vegetables, emotion swelling her syllables so they sometimes jiggled, and I heard and I saw all the different ways the women here were using their hands to break free from violence.

To the firing range. Because the Turkish president was threatening to attack Rojava, I was asked through hints and suggestions but not with specific words to provide something beyond self-defense training, just in case. In the dehydrated plains, I placed some rotting watermelons, a few decorated with slogans such as "I still like beer," or "Boys and girls and alcohol just don't mix," that I had written with a Sharpie, and a few others on which I had drawn pictures such as golf clubs or bags of money, and one with a generic, bearded man-face, for target practice. With two old rifles, I trained ten Kurdish, Arabic, Armenian, and Yazidi women how to duck and roll, and point and shoot, and hit a target with varying degrees of accuracy, which would prove later to be useful. When they asked me how I had learned to shoot like that, I explained that it was the kind of skill best learned on the job. One of the Yazidi women, a girl by American standards, who was well-liked and smiley, who had built her own house and tended her own garden, and whose handicrafts were quite popular at My Sister's Shop, cried so hard when she pulled the trigger that I felt fraudulent. During my time there, this girl would talk about the attack on Sinjar, and talk around her capture by ISIS, and talk in pieces of her sale at the sex slave market, and talk at length about her everyday life under the Caliphate, but would not talk at all about the child she had left behind in Raqqa. That was the kind of story you heard from someone else.

Road Trip in War Time

At the shared-ride taxi garage in Zakho, Kurdistan, there were three Special Forces soldiers exhilarated by a weekend R&R pass to Erbil. As they swung into the white pickup truck, they slapped each other's backsides and took bets on getting laid. They were rowdy and buoyant with alcohol, brazen after months of battling ISIS, and they wanted the regular people, the civilians, to know they had cheated death and now intended to relish life because they belonged to a singular, more heroic world.

There was a dirtier, duller truck behind, specifically chosen for its nondescript appeal. Inside were two men of the kind who always seem to be crisscrossing the border, the men with brown clothes, skin, teeth and with black, nylon duffel bags, who could be any age, with lined foreheads and silent, interchangeable faces, devout chins. They sit with their legs sprawled; an arm slung over a seatback. They keep a casual eye on their duffels stacked in the truck bed or on the driver, or they take turns shutting their eyes and going to sleep.

Wrapped in *kaffiyehs*, layered between prayer mats and rolled within multi-color carpets lay bootleg bottles of spirits and wine, and cartons of cigarettes to be smuggled through the Kurdish border town of Zakho on their way to Turkey or Iraq. Because ISIS had destroyed the distilleries in Mosul, smuggling alcohol into Iraq was now profitable; smuggling cigarettes had always been lucrative. The men smoke furiously in Kurdistan where the cigarettes are cheap, then abstain in Turkey so they don't burn through their profits.

The driver was weathered, with a Kalashnikov riding shotgun and a sidearm tucked into the large sash holding up his baggy pants. He could shuffle through phrases of English, Arabic, and Kurdish as the ethnicity of the checkpoint guards demanded. He might flash a Visa card if a guard looked hostile, or illiterate, because it's accepted anywhere you don't want to be. Professionally discreet, the driver kept an eye on the other cars and trucks waiting for fares in the dusty parking lot, and not on the passengers through the rearview mirror, which was strung with worry beads.

A western woman who had travelled a great deal by taxi, train, and plane debated which truck to climb into. She took in the wind-wrecked mountains surrounding the taxi garage as the drunken hoots of the Special Forces soldiers bounced off the limestone. She moved toward the front of the second truck, having decided to pay more to sit in the front seat, but then stopped. The Kalashnikov. The woman looked into the back seat. Neither man shifted. Either would probably make her climb over him and sit in the middle. The woman handed the driver the bloated fare, circled the hood, opened the front door, and climbed in, straddling the rifle in order to sit down, then closed the door. As she reached to adjust the weapon to a less suggestive position, the driver grabbed her wrist and threw it back at her. The barrel passed inches from her nose as he shoved it under her seat, his hand knocking her knee. She set her backpack between them to set some boundaries.

The truck rolled slowly to the exit and hiccupped to a stop. An advancing soldier escorted another passenger wearing a baseball cap. The brown men in the back seat looked at each other before the one sitting behind the woman poked her shoulder. No, she said without turning around. She hunkered down and fastened the chalky seatbelt. Too bad, she said to herself as she closed her eyes. I paid for it. There's no f-ing way I'm moving so your friend can accidentally feel me up every time this asshole behind the wheel hits a pothole. She was startled by a knock on the window behind her. The soldier was gesturing for the man behind her to move over. The soldier opened the passenger side door, and the newcomer folded his tall, leggy frame into the backseat.

The truck pulled onto the service road and turned to face the mountain before it began its slow assent, protesting under the weight of its load. The driver teased the gas pedal, cooing to the engine in Kurdish, encouraging the truck forward when it hesitated and the wheels slipped, feeding it more gas, hunching up over the steering wheel, petting the dash. No matter how many times you had driven this road, no matter the weather, the gravel, the rocks, the wild animals, ISIS bandits or sniper fire, your heart held until you reached the peak, and the view from the clouds stole your breath, and your stomach bounced to your toes as the truck slalomed down.

"That's-ah so nice," the man in the baseball cap said to himself. "A drive like a gasp, eh?"

The woman opened one eye. The rough-hewn rock shale on either side of the narrow road was a constant reminder of who was boss in the Middle Euphrates River Valley.

The man in the baseball cap looked at the other two men in the back seat, one of whom was looking out the window while the other was watching the driver's eyes in the rearview mirror. From the edge of conversation, the leggy man leaned forward. "You don't often see a woman travelling by herself here." His spoken English lilted and then swung.

"You do in my country." The woman pulled her scarf up over her face. She could feel how he wanted to talk, either to practice his English or to hit on her. She would only have to turn her head and smile, or say I know, letting her voice alpine, or say, it's not so bad, with prefabricated modesty; most anything would do. But she was not going to give him the satisfaction of being flattered by his momentary attention so he could talk about himself all the way to Erbil. I have three hours, she said in her head, aggressively, and they are mine, and it's not my responsibility to keep you entertained until you go home to your wife or your girlfriend or your mistress. The man watched the woman through the sideview mirror as she pulled her scarf over her entire face like a shade drawn. He pulled an electronic cigarette from his pocket and smoked, looking out the window.

Her rudeness faintly nagged at her though he had probably already forgotten it. She opened her eyes under her scarf and recalled his lanky frame walking towards the truck. She had seen him without really looking; his rangy build, his unhurried stride, that baseball cap. He was probably balding. His jeans were faded, his grey hoodie and navy thermal were nondescript. His olive skin bristled with a few days' stubble accenting his generous mouth. He carried a small backpack, which had hung casually from his shoulder and now lay between his feet on the floor of the truck. With resentment, because she did not want to be thinking about him, she yanked the scarf from her face and took out her phone. She opened the camera app and switched its view as if to take a selfie, so she could see his face without being observed. He was smoking an electronic cigarette, watching as the truck left the rough-hewn rock mountains and entered a poverty of landscape. His smoking face was a hangdog face, disconnected from the musicality of his voice. He cupped the e-cigarette in his large hand as if he were hiding it from himself and kept his gaze trained out the window. His brown eyes were shallow-lidded, made more sunken by the swollen, dark circles cupping them. His nose protruded slightly, fattening at the tip, drawing attention to the half-moon of his upper mouth. His neck was long and smooth in contrast to the thick hair bristling the edges of his cheeks and chin. Looped around his neck was a leather cord, whatever was hanging from it was hidden beneath the faded neckline of the blue thermal. Abruptly, he turned his head from the window. The woman fumbled her phone, which fell back behind her seat.

Shit, she said to herself, half turning to creep her hand around the damp and pebbled floor. She snatched up her phone before he could, lest he pick it up and see a version of himself. She wiped the phone on her jacket and threw it back in her bag. Let him smoke with his hangdog face. Let tobacco tar his warm-ocean voice. Let nicotine fray the smooth glide of his operatic vowels into the nubby worn of an old bathrobe. What do I care? By God, it was an irritating contradiction. How a voice could curve rich and melodic from an epicurean mouth anchored in such a browbeaten face.

Was she always this defensive, the man wondered behind his downcast face as he watched her childish hands scrabble for her phone. The phone's front screen was veined with cracks, and he could imagine her throwing it at a wall, this woman who was all lipstick and dare. She didn't look like the type of woman who was contrary all the time. Pretty women usually got their way, especially pretty, foreign women, especially here, and she must know that because she wore makeup. As he had approached the truck, there had been a flicker of recognition, in that vague way good-looking people acknowledge one another when they pass each other in the street. She had taste if not money; her black leather jacket was stylish, though one shoulder was held together with electrical tape. Beneath her jacket she wore an ambitiously green dress, the wrong clothes for the context, and she wore them without concern. She sounded American, was probably an English teacher or a disaster tourist, entitled, as they all were, or bored with life, as they all were, and bent on having a profound experience before she returned home to set herself up in a cookie cutter suburb. But her face was better than most. He did not think of women as pretty or not pretty, exclusively. He simply thought her face was exotic; it was oval and smooth and lively with thick penciled eyebrows over very large, very green eyes. There were big rings on both forefingers, which drew attention to her nails, which were short and faintly dirty beneath their half-hearted varnish. Her cuticles were rough, and in sharp contrast to the precision with which she had made up her face, doer hands, worker hands, and he liked this best about her. Defensive as hell, he smiled to himself. Then he forgot her.

He relaxed into the ride, thinking of how much closer he was towards reaching the project's first milestone than he had been two days ago when he arrived at the US military base housed in an old cement factory. So far, the higher-ups were pleased with his work though the next step would be more challenging. By deploying Niometrix's full-stack system into a country's mobile telecommunications network, those with access would be able to track and monitor the behavior data of any citizen on that network. Niometrix would need to retain full access after the system was up and running because the deep state wanted to manipulate the users' future behavior, so his next task was to convince the mobile telecommunications company to give him full access to every mobile phone user's behavior data. He thought the burgeoning protests over government corruption in the south might work to his advantage. When the next milestone is completed, he thought in the warm-water voice he didn't know he had, he was done. He'd cash out and leave Niometrix, leave the Middle East and start living again. He had been in the field for eleven years, in places like Afghanistan, India, Malaysia, Indonesia, and the Philippines, places where societal future behavior needed to be influenced, places where telecommunications needed to be monitored to mine behavior data undetected. He didn't contemplate the ethics of his job because he didn't believe in a moral high ground. There was only power. Data was power and money was freedom, so he was unperturbed by trading data for money to gain freedom.

He had owned a string of small computer shops before he joined Niometrix, but he did not want to be a man with a computer shop again. It wouldn't be as nice as it had been back then, when things were simpler, when the internet was a visionary novelty and access to information was an equalizer, not an instrument for control. People from all walks of life were connecting with one another as if everyone on the planet had been invited to the same global party, enjoying the fun. There had been a lot of women, a lot of drugs, specifically coke, and he remembered how hard it had been to kick the habit, even with Petros' help, so now he had no interest in it. What he wanted next was simplicity. He listened to the bath water voice inside his head remind him of how well things had gone yesterday and how well things would continue to go. There was next week's celebration party at the company's HQ in Singapore, where no expense would be spared. He and Petros would gamble, shoot pool, and enjoy the nightlife with two beauties for a couple of days before he returned to northern Iraq and worked towards the project's next milestone. When he reached it, he'd take his payout and go to an island where he'd swim and surf, and maybe open a fried fish shack right on the beach. He stretched his legs under the truck seat in front of him and felt how well things would go washing over him like salt water in sunlight.

A kick under the woman's seat jolted her from the verge of sleep. She sat up and bowed her head, shaking it from side to side to loosen her neck. She pulled the ponytail holder from around her bun and her dark hair unfolded around her face before she settled back into her seat and silently cursed him for waking her. Why couldn't he have ridden with the Special Forces, she thought, unless he's a private security contractor. I bet he works for Academi or Triple Canopy or some other right-wing mercenary group employed by the government to legitimize killing under the guise of security. The woman recalled the rumors of a US military base housed inside an old cement factory near the taxi garage. Now his appearance made sense. The baseball cap and hoodie made him look like one of them and therefore one they could trust. But his backpack was small, geared for a quick in and out. He probably kept a glass box of an apartment in Dubai or Istanbul, modern and luxurious, to function as a base for his regular R&R, and another home, an apartment in Europe or a house in the States, where a wife and some kids lived. The security contractors she knew from the consulate compound and military bases were all the same; young to relatively young, making more money than they knew how to spend. They ran up big tabs in small bars or ordered everything on the menu at the overpriced, mediocre restaurants that sprang up in the neighborhoods where expats lived. The existence of contractors could mean something or nothing; contractors were used to take the State Department folks to Carrefour, where the contractors walked nobly behind non-essential personnel through aisles of personal hygiene products and condoms, muttering into their earpieces. They escorted UN experts to think tank symposiums, where they stood by the refreshments table, eyeing pistachio nut cookies, muttering into their earpieces. There was, for example, the ex-marine Morale, Welfare and Recreation Specialist who now worked as a contractor guarding the back entrance of the US consulate compound. He lived in expensive lackluster on the compound, where the security company he worked for charged the US tax-payer by way of the Department of State $42 for each of his three daily meals at one of the compound's two restaurants. She had known him for a little while, knew he pulled in over six figures for a few hours' work a day, but probably knew less about security threats in the region than she did. So, what the existence of a new contractor not tied to an embassy or a UN agency in the region meant, she did not know. She thought again about the man's unremarkable attire, his essentials-only backpack. If he were a security contractor, his being here would mean something. His probable wife would be reliably at home, worrying about him as she packed school lunches or checked math homework, praying for his safety in her lonely bed, but also very proud, why shouldn't she be? The woman was annoyed at herself. She didn't have a problem with wives, per se, but she did not share their interests, especially if they had children. She likened being a mother to being suffocated, though still quite alive, so you felt your truest part dying as your life became a series of routines organized around someone else's convenience. She could hear her ex, Marcus, now, and her chest tightened with pity and rage. How do you expect me to support you going to Iraq? He spat. Would you support me if I wanted to jump out of that tree? And then, later, I love you more than anything and I don't want to lose you. In that moment, Marcus believed what he said while she felt cold, and trapped and guilty, because she didn't believe it at all. The woman groaned and twisted herself into a sideways heap, but the seat back smelled of sweat and stale breath so she untwisted herself onto her back, saying to herself it's done, it's done. You cannot know why you loved a man, nor why you no longer love him, or if love and ego are always mutually exclusive. It's not a crime to want something of my own, she told herself. I will not have a small life, she vowed, and lulled by the wheels rolling over the minutes between miles, she fell back asleep.

She flops like a fish in a frying pan, the man chuckled as he watched the woman's body helix, straighten, then settle in the sideview mirror. Her face was active in rest; eyelids twitching until her mouth fell open, emitting a faint snore. The truck rolled past herds of sheep searching for sustenance in the desolate fields, and her snoring became part of the truck sounds. As he watched her, his eyelids grew heavier and finally closed. His brooding face quieted into an uncertain serenity swathed in an anticipation of being disturbed. In his sleep, he did not dream but went to a specific place, a tiny rock of dark earth surround by dark water under dark air.

Both the air and water had weight, so he was trapped within the darkness, waiting to be either recovered or destroyed. His elbows anchored themselves onto the rock to keep his head and chest in the dark air while the rest of him hung in the dark, weighty water. He could not see his forearms on the rock or where the rock ended and the water began, or where the air met the water because the darkness was complete, like blindness. He felt it. The air was the heaviest, and he was under it; immobile but buoyed by the water, which was also strong, so that his body kept a ballast between the above and the below.

He lay there every time he slept, and when he woke he was always surprised yet suspicious, though he did not know why, because he did not remember the darkness in which he had been sleeping.

This sleeping in opaque, yin-yang darkness had started gradually during his military service, after his rescue from an islet in the grey zone of undetermined sovereignty between Turkey and Greece. He and two compatriots had been sent to the islet, which was more uninhabited rock than island, to protect the Greek flag mounted there. Despite the febrile tension caused by flags on rocks, he was confident because he had been raised with that particular blend of privilege and freedom that builds assurance. He knew himself, recognized he was lucky because he did all right without really trying, and had no reason to think he would not continue being lucky. When the supply ship missed its weekly restock and they had to ration food and water, he didn't worry. When the attack came and his compatriots were killed, he believed he would survive. He hid in the water to evade Turkish forces for twenty-four cold and hungry hours before he was rescued. Lucky.

There was another time when he was having a breakfast meeting in a Kabul hilltop hotel popular with foreigners and journalists. Outlining the swimming pool were tables clothed in white linen surrounded by red-cushioned, gold-rimmed straight back chairs set against six-meter high pine trees whose fairy lights made shrapnel in the shrubbery. He sat at one of the poolside tables across from the CEO of a privately-held Afghan telecom company that had just received a fifty-million-dollar World Bank grant and a twenty-five-year license to provide fixed line, wireless voice and data services throughout the country. He seemed to have nothing to do in this meeting but watch the CEO puff out his chest as they drank the endless glasses of sugary green tea usually required for these types of negotiations. The tea drinking was, of course, symbolic, since the telecom company's receiving the grant was contingent upon the telecom company's accepting the Niometrix system. The CEO lifted his tea glass towards his white-haired chin terribly slowly, a slim gold band pinching the skin of his swollen ring finger. Invisible drawstrings pulled the CEO's lips into a tight O as he blew on his tea, slowly. Faint streams of steam wisped, slowly. The man watched the CEO's lips rim his tea glass, slowly, because he had never had so much time and so little to do. This must have lasted only a few seconds, but the seconds stretched fat and large and held until gunmen burst through the pine trees, disturbing their fairy lights.

The CEO's blimped ring finger was found lodged in the corner of the top rung of the swimming pool ladder, kept fresh by the chlorinated water. The leggy man did not see this because the gunmen hooded him and then pulled him from his red-cushioned chair, which toppled over onto the white marble patio tiles. As his hands were zipped-tied behind his back, he recalled the US Army-style uniforms worn by the gunmen, probably purchased at Bush Bazaar. He was pulled firmly but not roughly back through the pine trees, the fairy lights shining votive against the needle leaves. Time sped up. His captors hustled him to a waiting car. A hand palmed the crown of his head and pushed down as his body collapsed into the waiting jaws of an open trunk. He heard the lid slam shut, making the darkness under his hood darker, muffling sound as if he were under water, and he felt the back of the car sink down and then rise up as his kidnappers settled into the back and front seats, and the vehicle buoyed. He reasoned there were four of them, the typical number for a smash and grab unit, provided there were strategically placed loyalists in the concerned institutions, which in this case included the telecom company, the hotel and its restaurant staff and security, and the traffic police, all micromanaged from the top down. He thought about his own taxi driver, who was also his fixer. You had to wonder if he was in on it, if he had been coerced or bribed since that was how things were generally done in places where Niometrix was called to set up its system. Most likely the Taliban had taken him, and the reason he was not bleeding on a crimson-cushioned, gold-framed, pool side chair was that he had something they wanted—lucky.

The dusty car, an American Corolla from the late '90s, boasting an Ahmad Shah Massoud sticker, sped its way down the hillside towards the chaos of the inner city, where it got caught in the stop-and-roll of downtown Kabul traffic. The phlegmy cough of a motorcycle rattled past the man in the trunk's head, and he imagined a motorcycle driver ivy-ing his way through a multi-lane gridlock of vehicles. When the car coasted in a semi-circle, he reasoned they had entered Abdul Haq Square roundabout, not far from the US Embassy. A series of short, quick turns across potholed corners jostled the man's body much like an amateur surfer being surprised by rogue waves. The car halted and four doors opened and then slammed shut before the trunk popped up and sunlight cut the darkness. A rush of cool air tickled the hem of skin between the hood and the man's unbuttoned shirt collar. From somewhere came the shouts of children playing. He was pushed to a sitting position, then lifted by his armpits and ankles to standing. From nearby wafted the scent of grilled corn. He was urged along broken and uneven concrete until the hot sun knifing the top of his head disappeared. A jangle of keys. A door scraped open, and he was pushed inside a building, tripped up three flights of stairs, rushed down a short hallway through another door, down another hallway, and into a room. The hood was swapped for a blindfold during which time he registered a lime green painted wall, a single bare window, and a red geometric-patterned rug over a faux hardwood floor. His hands remained zip-tied behind his back. He was led to a cushioned area along a wall where he was helped to kneel and then sit. When a plastic rectangle of water was brought to the man's lips, he knew he would live.

"*Shukran,*" the man said because he did not know the Dari word for "thank you."

When he was slapped, the man knew not to speak again.

A door clicked shut. From outside came the midday call to prayer. The man ignored the ache in his face and shoulder sockets and thought about what had happened and what difference it would make going forward. They probably wanted the access codes, which was both easy and difficult. If he had to, he would give them up. He felt no allegiance to a deep state that had coerced Petros into forming Niometrix so it could control the market place for behavioral futures. However, he would not be able to give them working access codes until the entire system was deployed and functional, and given that the man in charge of the telecom company was most likely dead, deploying Niometrix' full-stack system would, most likely, be delayed. The man resigned himself to being wherever he was for a while, for being taken had already happened, and now what he had to do was survive. Time would pass, and he would stay alive, and that was all there was to it. In the end, he stayed in blindfolded darkness for thirty days, giving up the access codes shortly before he was found and freed by his taxi driver.

Still, every night, he went to a layered, counterbalanced darkness, where he was eternally interred, without sound or sight or anyone to talk to.

The truck rolled to a stop at the checkpoint near Mosul. The driver gathered everyone's identity cards to present to a *Pesh Merga* soldier as another swept the underside of the truck with a mirror attached to a long metal stick and a third half-heartedly checked the cargo. The soldier who took the identity cards returned without them, telling the driver to pull off onto the shoulder of the road just beyond the guard house and gather his passengers outside the truck. The driver caught one of the smuggler's eyes in the rearview mirror and listened as the smuggler's eyes did the talking before grabbing his worry beads. The leggy foreigner wiped the sides of his mouth before he looped his backpack over his shoulder and opened his car door. The woman draped her scarf over the top of her head, crisscrossing the ends over either shoulder and exited. The smugglers and the driver followed.

The driver stood nearest to the guard house clicking his worry beads as the two smugglers smoked nearby. Now in the great outdoors, the leggy man abandoned his e-cigarette and interrogated his pockets for a real smoke. Locating a pack, he withdrew it and offered a cigarette to the woman. "Women smoke in your country."

"I don't." The woman hugged herself a little. On either side of the road, low, brownish-green hills yawned in every direction.

"Do you mind?" The man indicated the cigarette in his hand.

"What if I said yes?" The woman looked directly at him. "Would you not smoke it?"

"No, but I'd move away,"

"Then, yes." She smiled as she said it.

The man nodded his head and joined the other smoking men. They stood companionably, one tall and two small, not talking to one another, a solar system of smoke above their heads.

Although she had sent him away, the woman felt disappointment when he went. No guts, no glory, she thought and trained her gaze on the private cars and taxis whizzing through the checkpoint. Bored, she walked towards the guard house to peer inside the window. Her identity card was on a desk where a soldier leaned, talking on the phone. As she approached, he moved to block her view. She veered towards the group of smoking men, keeping one eye on the guard house door, which was ajar.

"I thought you minded," the man said in his bubble bath voice.

"You're almost done," The woman looked at his wonderfully soft mouth rather than his eyes, which were shaded by the brim of his baseball cap.

He flicked his butt to the ground.

The woman glanced at the guard house. "I wonder what the problem is."

"Maybe there's no problem. Maybe it's just the way things are."

The woman hesitated, letting his warm water voice wash over her, softening her sharp tongue, slipping sounds into her throat. She was about to say her name and ask for his when a soldier came out of the guard house with their identity cards and handed them to their owners, pausing to give the woman one long, last look before returning hers. The woman stared back as she pocketed her ID and then tailed the driver and the leggy man back to the truck. The two smugglers smoked their cigarettes to the filter before they returned, indifferent to the others waiting. Back on the road, the truck began to smell close, pungent with bodies and old cigarette smoke. The woman cranked the truck window handle, but the window didn't budge. She sighed audibly and asked the driver with gestures more than with words to open his window a bit, which he ignored. When he pulled off the highway and onto a road leading to the outskirts of Mosul, she protested again, which he again ignored. Fuming, she curtly reminded him they were to go to Erbil, not Mosul, and he should have told her about the detour before he had accepted her fare.

"He doesn't understand you," the leggy man was rolling down his window when the driver tsssked him. "Come onna. Justa little." His voice swayed with the ebb and flow of the road.

"I know, but it makes me feel better saying it. He knows he shouldn't be taking westerners this close to Mosul." She spat her words at the driver before turning her head to catch the feather of a breeze coming through the leggy man's cracked window.

"Are you always this defensive?"

"That's about as helpful as telling a woman to smile." She turned forward, leaving further conversation to tremble on his lips.

The woman's experience was that being female in the Middle East was at best an imposition. Never mind the inconvenience of squatter toilets; it was the cloak of invisibility in professional settings which infuriated her. In debriefings, male colleagues solicited one another's opinions as they debated neo-con ideals in typical blowhard fashion, her existence acknowledged only as eye candy. Come onna! Realizing she was mimicking the melodic wave of the leggy man's bathwater voice, she rolled her eyes, and rested her forehead in her palm. She replaced the tide of his words with smoky jazz, a haunting refrain riding the frayed edge between grief and regret. Without thinking, she hummed a few lapping, mournful bars, drifting. The truck hit a deep pothole and swerved, jolting its passengers, severing her song. The truck thundered into and then out of another street cavity as the driver swerved to avoid the burnt-out carcass of an abandoned car. As a third crater sent their heads towards the truck's ceiling, a firm hand landed between the woman's shoulder and her clavicle. Another concrete pocket ejected them skyward, and the hand slipped across her right breast. Paused in an unlikely connection, the hand removed itself as the driver regained control of the truck. The woman whipped around in her seat as the leggy man issued an apology and explanation; he had been trying to protect her head. She stared furiously; her face heated. Facing forward, she realized she had liked the feel of his hand on her breast, its quiet assurance through the thin leather of her coat, and she wanted him to touch her again, to lay his owning hands possessively, to demand her. The woman swallowed, pressing her lips together in a firm, hard line before she trained her gaze on the mounds of pulverized rubble banking the road.

A brief moment of accidental touch brought into focus her months of gnawing unlove. At that moment, the other passengers in the truck did not matter. All the woman wanted was for the leggy man to seize her, to kiss her as if they were already lovers, because she wanted to belong to someone and someone to belong to her instead of being misunderstood and adrift in a destroyed and hopeless world.

As the truck approached the eastern side of Mosul, the signs of war abated. Squat, rectangular buildings, largely intact, crowded along streets veined with cracks. The sound of birds returned. The driver turned into a residential area with trees but few leaves and parked near a man in a wheelchair selling watermelons from the back of a pickup truck. Across from the makeshift fruit stand was a schoolyard, where forty or so middle school boys ovalled around another boy in an olive-colored sweater and black jeans, shooting a free throw. Hanging on a schoolyard wall behind the players was a colorful poster of an exploding IED, warning people not to touch suspicious objects.

After a few minutes, a schoolyard supervisor backed up toward the street, keeping an eye on the playing children. When he neared the wall, he glanced at the truck, pulled a phone from his pocket and messaged someone. Inside the truck, one of the smugglers' phones beeped. The smuggler directed the driver towards a mosque at the corner of a nearby intersection, where he turned and parked in front of a small convenience store. A teenage girl in faded blue jeans, a black sweater and a grey hijab leaned against a cardboard kiosk selling Dalya brand snack chips. As the truck parked, she put four fingers into her mouth and wolf whistled. A minute later, a white Kia pulled up, and the teenage girl rushed to open its backseat doors before walking to the intersection to serve as a lookout. The two smugglers offloaded their carpets and black, nylon duffels into the Kia. When the task was finished, one smuggler got into the front passenger seat of the Kia, which sped off. The second smuggler handed some money to the young girl before he disappeared into the labyrinth of streets surrounding the mosque, and the truck carrying the woman and the leggy man drove away.

"Not even-ah time for a cigarette," the leggy man unfolded his long limbs across the floor of the backseat as he watched the teenage girl walk back to the kiosk.

"They were quick," agreed the woman as she typed into her phone.

There was a long stretch of silence before the leggy man shook his head and chuckled.

"What's so funny?" asked the woman although she did not turn and look at him.

"That-ah small girl had such-ah big whistle."

The woman pictured the girl's tightly fastened hijab, not a seam of hair exposed. The pressure of being contained. "Doesn't surprise me at all." The woman slid her phone into her bag and watch the mosque recede in the distance.

"Why not?"

"Maybe it's the only chance she gets to express herself."

"Come onna."

"I mean it. All the frustration and rage of being deemed less than or worse yet, invisible, because of what's between your legs. Perhaps that whistle is her release."

"Why are you here?"

"Right now, I am enjoying a luxury mode of transportation, same as you. How's that leg room?"

The man in the back seat slouched and sprawled. "First class."

"Would you mind if I moved my seat back?" the woman addressed him from over her shoulder.

"What if I said yes?" the man teased.

"I wouldn't move it," the woman lied. "But since you're okay with it," her hand fumbled on the side of her seat and then under it, looking for a lever. When she didn't find one, she asked the driver, who ignored her. "See what I mean?" The woman turned her head and looked at the man. He had pushed back his baseball cap, better revealing his eyes, which were bright despite the teaspoons of shadow under them. "Why are you here?"

"I'm here for work."

"May I ask what you do?"

"I work in telecommunications. You?"

"Research."

"What kind of research?"

"Currently, the recycling of war scrap in post-ISIS Iraq."

The leggy man's laugh was an echo in a deep well.

"What's so funny?"

"You look like-ah this and you research-ah that."

The woman bit her lip. "What do you do in telecom?"

"Mobile advertising."

Data and behavior. She arranged her face into an expression which lulled men into thinking they had your full attention, but you weren't smart enough to follow what they were saying. "Which company?" There were three main players in the region, each allied with a rival political party, which were in bed with different proxy governments. Knowing whom he was working for would hint at which external stakeholder was directing him.

The man's eyes clouded. Behind her carefully applied makeup, he detected a schism. In response, he used silence, wielding it better than words.

The woman shifted in her seat to stretch her neck. "Those smugglers were something. In a parallel universe, they oil their beards and keep books of erotic Chinese lithographs, which they invite women over to see."

This time his laugh was a drum. The man's eyes cleared and the woman realized she liked looking into them. "What? A thought just crossed your mind."

"How did you know?"

"Your eyes are transparent." The woman turned all the way round in her seat and perched on her knees, anchoring her elbows over the seatback.

"I was thinking I should invite you to sit-ah in the back seat, so you wouldn't strain your neck."

The woman took that as she needed it. "That's very considerate of you." Her eyes had gone soft, almost loving. She rested her chin on her hands and let the moment cross accidentally into sincere.

He watched her sad, sly, seductive face.

They stayed eye-locked in silence, their separate thoughts curling around them like water, as they futured themselves into separate scenes. The woman saw them in a tangle of bed sheets, morning sunlight breaking through the blinds covering the windows. In a post-coital haze, they lazed, beautiful, sharing a newspaper. There would be soft kisses and caresses, the prelude to another bodily feasting on loamy sheets before a late morning shower, brunch, and then a stroll through the bazaar, where he'd offer to buy her a trinket, some mass-produced ethnic ornament made to look artisan. She'd refuse, but he'd buy it anyway. Then, they would lie together again, and she would make it mean everything she wanted him to think. The man thought about the peace and quiet of his luxury hotel room, how he would order a thick steak from room service, and enjoy all the alcoholic contents of the mini bar while he sat alone in a plush bathrobe on his hotel room balcony, smoking real cigarettes as a blue-black dark palmed the tired and run-down city.

The woman looked at his assured lips, well-suited for more than the task of language, and sighed. There was nothing further she could do about him now, riding backwards in a truck, with the driver probably staring at her ass. The moment, alone of its kind, had happened without announcement or reason, and was now dissipating like the rippled undulations of a stone skipped into water. It would be fruitless to grasp at a shifting version of the present. She unhooked her elbows and turned to face front. The low, rolling brown hills mottled with shriveled vegetation had given way to a quarry of one and two-story concrete buildings set off from the highway.

The driver peeled his eyes from the woman's backside in time to brake hard and avoid hitting a white Hyundai trying to exit right from the left lane. The worry beads swung violently from the rearview mirror as the driver swerved. Silently, he cursed the woman. These foreigners were all the same.

Outside the windshield, the sky asked for sunset. The driver slowed as the small grey-green of the Erbil city checkpoint loomed ahead. He braked again at the checkpoint entrance as a soldier peered inside the truck, noted the western faces, and waved the truck through. The driver bungled over a speed bump to join the stop-start domino cue of vehicles waiting to pass the entrance to Family Mall. Behind the mall, the Family Fun Ferris Wheel spun whorls of rainbow-colored sherbet light in the dusty air.

Dismissed by the turn of her body, the man felt a mixture of relief and confusion and disappointment and thirst. He tried to think about the fine time he and Petros would have in Singapore, the fresh, uncomplicated beauties, and the smooth, warm pleasurable nights, but the memory of the woman's face perched atop the seatback distracted him. She had fine lips, twin pillows ready to part, and if he had been a different kind of man, he would have sat up and kissed them, but he was used to being lucky in life and not having to try. There would be plenty of lips to kiss in Singapore; Petros was sure to arrange it. The type of woman who smiled a lot and said little and left by morning. It had been years since he had known another type of woman, because it was easier this way. The man rummaged in his bag for a water bottle to unstick the loneliness bricking his throat.

"Want some?" the leggy man extended his water bottle forward.

The woman was scribbling in a notebook. She frowned as she shook her head but kept writing. "No, thanks." The words backflipped over her shoulder as her pen scratched furiously across the paper.

The driver looked at the water bottle. He was thirsty.

The leggy man's arm lingered and then withdrew to its ignorance. He had made a mistake about himself but did not know it. The man drained the bottle, crushed it, and then shoved it into his bag. The woman ignored the crackle of plastic crumpling, engrossed in her writing. There was the smuggling operation, which she had filmed on her phone. It could tie into her research on the scrap metal trade, which had been co-opted by the Hashd al-Sha 'abi as it vied for control over the post-conflict economy, or into the larger issue of corruption throughout Iraq's political and economic systems. Already, millions of tons of scrap had been taken from private homes, municipal buildings, and military equipment and hauled from Mosul to Erbil in an unregulated and legally ambiguous way, where it was sold far below market value with the complicity of local politicians and security actors. It was also being smuggled into Iran despite an official ban on the exportation of scrap metal. Then there was the leggy man himself, monitoring the user behavior of a country's telecommunications network, perhaps at the behest of a proxy government. The woman folded her lips under to keep from smiling.

The leggy man sat forward and rested his elbows behind each front seat head rest. "You look almost happy," he said to the woman. She had drawn a mind map across two open pages and was filling it in with the names of the usual suspects. The woman snapped her notebook shut.

"I am. You?" the notebook disappeared into her bag.

His head bobbed up and down. "Good." He said it as though he were convincing himself.

"You sure?" She was looking at him again from over her shoulder.

He swiped the baseball cap from his head and ran a hand over a buzzed peninsula of hair before replacing the cap and pulling it low over his eyes. "I want-ta get out-ta this truck and smoke." The truck turned into the parking lot of the Erbil Garage, where other shared taxis seemed to block their way on purpose.

"Soon enough." The woman gathered her things.

The truck rolled to the rank and parked. The leggy man and the woman exited together. "Where-ah are you headed?" the leggy man withdrew a cigarette from his crumpled pack.

"Ainkawa. You?"

"Divan Erbil."

The woman rubbed her eyes. "How long have you been here?"

"Four months. You?"

"Seems like forever." Living in a luxury hotel meant deep pockets. It also meant she knew where to find him. She wondered who was funding him. "Well, good luck to you." The woman crossed the parking lot to the street, where she hailed a local taxi. The man watched her wave at him from behind her back without looking at him as she got into the car.

The woman settled into the backseat of the taxi with her pen and notebook. All the ideas that had been running through her head now dried up.

Sighing, she glanced out the window and saw the leggy man standing on the street, smoking. For a moment, he seemed to look directly at her.

She coughed and opened her phone to review the day's footage. Caught between turns of the smugglers running carpets from the truck bed into the Kia's backseat was the leggy man's face, filling the frame. He smiled as if he were rooting for the smugglers. The woman paused the video to linger on his full lips, tracing his long, smooth neck with a fingertip. She could have invited him to share her taxi, and perhaps they would have had some fun or something more than fun. Instead, she had chosen her work, and in turn, inspiration deserted her.

The man stood on the uncomplicated street, smoking his fine cigarette, and watched the woman's taxi be eaten up by the ring road's rush hour. He relished his cigarette, erasing the woman, until the smoke dissipated and they both were finished and gone.

V

THE SYMBOL OF KURDISH HOPE FLASHES HER V FOR VICTORY SIGN in a photo that goes viral. She has killed a hundred ISIS militants outside Kobani, and now she is hot, hot, hot. Her pseudonym is Rehana and her sisters-in-arms have been trading kitchen cutlery for Kalashnikovs ever since Chemical Ali chased the Kurds up the hill with his toxoid apple gas. Sabiha Sahar, in the computer room of the Oakland Public Library, peers at the photo so closely her nose touches the screen. Her heavy hair grapevines the keyboard. Rehana's not just about defending the Kurdish homeland: she fought to keep women from being locked in their houses, for Chrissake. She thinks they should have been sisters, thousands of miles and another world apart. At least she'd know the basics of star navigation or how to shoot a gun. Sabiha is a caged bird who wants her home to be the sky.

The ten thousand strong female battalion, the *Peshmergettes*, she reads, has a female chain of command, including its own chief. In the photo, Rehana wears matching camouflage pants and shirt, her hips neatly defined by an ammo belt. An upside-down middle finger salute steadies the rifle at her side. She looks like a sexy GI Jane doll, her streaked blond hair loosely braided down her back. Sabiha wears a baggy black shirt over a shapeless long black skirt. While she reads, her nimble fingers weave her hair. When the braid is finished, Sabiha stares past Rehana, at the edges of her, to blur Rehana's face so their in-commons become keener.

In her mind's eye, Sabiha unbuttons the camouflage shirt and sees plastic-doll smooth skin. She buffs the light tan color with the pad of her thumb until Rehana gleams alabaster.

White girls get to do more than brown girls, but no girl gets to do more than a boy. Boys are always on top, right? So there's always a problem if you're the kind of girl who wants to do stuff. Sabiha wants to do *a lot* of stuff, all at the same time, but she doesn't know what exactly, which sidelines her eager self.

Sabiha reads on. In the nineteenth century, Kara Fatma led a battalion of seven hundred men in the Ottoman Empire and stuck forty-three women into the army ranks. It's the twenty-first century and Sabiha's brother doesn't let her wear makeup to high school. She keeps Wet Ones in her book bag so she can wipe it off before she takes the afternoon bus home. Let's not talk about the skinny jeans she hides in her school locker.

The dead-leaf crinkle of tinfoil scratches her ear. A girl in a gray hijab and chador coughs as she finishes unwrapping a sandwich hidden in her lap. A petticoat of lettuce swirls around the edges. Sabiha hits control/print and saunters to the beat of invisible club music to the front of the room. She positions herself in the sight line between Hijab and Chador and the computer room supervisor and strikes a pose. Hijab and Chador stares furiously at a half-filled notebook page as her mouth slow-motion chews. The supervisor hands Sabiha her printouts of the Rehana V photo and the *Peshmergettes*, which she safeguards in the side compartment of her bag. Hijab and Chador coughs again, and Sabiha *knows* she is balling the foil in her fist, squeezing the day's grievances into its forgiving shape. Outside the library windows, the evening is purpling. Inside Sabiha's head an electric guitar riffs twice. It sounds like a kaleidoscope of stars.

The city bus smells of Fritos and wet socks. Sabiha tucks her nose into her shirt collar and inhales her own girl smell. If her scent were music, it would be the honeyed melody of an oud flirting in toe shoes with a flute. Out of nowhere, dog-kiss raindrops slather the window panes. The Black Lives Matter protestors in Oscar Grant Plaza pop their hoodies or gather under scant awnings in clusters as complex as snowflakes. Sabiha graffities the glass with her fingertips. When she exits, a track of Vs stand *en pointe* in her wake.

As the wind catches it, the screen door bangs a samba, announcing Sabiha's arrival home. Her mother is making dinner with a phone cradled between her shoulder and ear. Her bones make a step ladder in her chest. When Sabiha hears her mother's swoon song of Kurdish, she knows the phone line stretches to Dubai, where her father spools out affection like kite string. The last time Sabiha spoke to him was seven months, twelve days, and four hours ago. Sabiha beats it to her bedroom.

Sirood enters without knocking. Ever since their father was transferred to the Emirates, her brother thinks it's his God given right to tell her what to do 'Where were you?' he demands and straddles her desk chair, resting his chalky elbows on its wooden back. Was it only last summer that she filmed his Ice Bucket challenge? He strokes his chin. He's so proud of his facial hair.

"It's still there. You can stop touching it."

"I asked you where you were."

Sabiha is Queen of the Dirty Look, which Sirood ignores. Fine. Practice makes perfect. "The LIE-brary."

"Sabiha, there are protests everywhere. I worry about you. We may have been born here, but people don't think we belong."

Sabiha mentally erases the boy-hair dirtying his upper lip, splotchy along his chin. Now Sirood is The Finder of Lost Toys, The Inventor of Games, The Prolonger of Bedtime Stories. She relents. "I know, but I'm careful. I'm almost fifteen." She sits up straighter.

"Exactly." Sirood's voice is dusty.

"Anyway, what do you think Dad wants?"

"What makes you think he wants something? He calls because he misses us."

"Yeah, that's why he talks to us." Sabiha reads the fine print of Sirood's face. "He talked to you?"

"Just for a second. Mostly to remind me to watch out for you."

Sirood's voice changes to a texture Sabiha can't name: velvet, sandpaper, rain. A lone saxophone wails in her head.

"I can watch out for myself."

"Okay tough girl. But the tougher ones are easier to hurt."

Now his voice is a cat weaving around her ankle. She decides not to fight him for the moment. "Why do you think Dad doesn't want to talk to me?"

Sirood doesn't thrive on tiny cruelties. "He wants to. You weren't home. He's real busy."

An ache opens in Sabiha's gut and spreads to her chest. *I'm home now.* "I don't care." She turns on her side and curls into a pill bug.

The chair scrapes the bare floor, and then Sirood is sitting on her bed, causing her body to tip slightly towards him. A hand warms her right shoulder. Sabiha shrugs it off. *They probably talk whenever I'm not around.* The silence they fall into has something hard at the bottom. Rain stamps the rooftop.

Jesse is a beefy boy with a Jesus-mane men twice his age would kill for. He'll be eighteen in four months and seven days and then it's *Fuck this place!* He's joining the Marines and high school won't ever be the same without him. Sabiha watches him from across the lunchroom, watches as he jabs the air with a French fry, talking about getting *hajis*, watches as his arm slips around his girlfriend's twiggy shoulders, disturbing her mermaid hair. His index finger twigs her nipple and a spark flies out and catches Sabiha in the eye, so she doesn't see a table full of faces swivel in her direction. It's only later, when she's settled in the library, does Sabiha realize *haji* was a dog whistle calling everyone to look at her.

Sabiha takes the photos of Rehana and the *Peshmergettes* out of her book bag. The battalion is a box of Whitman's Sampler with its top off: Rehana is as light as milky tea while some girls are as dark as polished oak. One or two are Jesse-white. Most of the people in the computer room are a Starbucks variety. Since when did Sabiha's world get thrown behind a sepia-toned viewfinder?

The door opens and Hijab and Chador snags on the doorframe before striding towards a trio of empty chairs keeping Sabiha company. The chador's hem sails out behind the girl's denim clad legs and flaps back to kiss her calves. A thought so crazy it seems sane crosses Sabiha's mind: they are destined to be friends.

Sit here. Sit here. Sit here. Sabiha closes her eyes to focus her inner magnetic pull. When she opens them, Hijab and Chador is lounging one computer away. Sabiha's aim has always been a little off.

Hijab and Chador slants her a look.

Sabiha smiles. This is going to be easier than she thought.

Hijab and Chador seals herself behind an arm wall. She hooks her thumb under her ear to cradle her head and surfs the web. Suddenly, she turns and laser-stares into Sabiha's pupils like she's going to drill a hole in her skull. "What do you want?" Hijab and Chador's voice is a brick wall.

What does she want? Sabiha wants to know why her father doesn't speak to her. She wants to know, when you kiss a boy, where the noses go. For just one day, she wants to be one of those girls whose clothes look like they are trying to flee their bodies. She wants her life to start already, and what's takin' it so flipping long? "What's your name?"

"Hiba." The two syllables come to Sabiha from across a long bridge.

"I'm Sabiha."

"Great. We done here?"

Hiba returns her face to her computer screen.

"I—"

Hiba doesn't break her typing. "Just because we're both sand niggers don't mean I wanna to talk to you. Now fuck off."

Sabiha tenses as if freezing water were being dumped down her back. Turning to her computer screen, she draws the curtain of her hair so Hiba can't see the magenta scribbling her cheeks. A spiral notebook slaps shut. A zipper rips closed. A chair scrapes away. One, two, three and Hiba is gone baby gone. A black and white *kaffiyeh* lies forgotten under her desk. Sabiha rescues the scarf and runs out of the computer room. No Hiba in the hallway. No Hiba in the lot outside. Sabiha feels the sidewalk pushing through her shoes. It propels her back into the computer room.

The page Hiba was looking at features honey-colored pancakes striped insouciant with syrup. Sabiha scrolls through pictures. The next snap frames a white egg lazing in a white square bowl on a '60s psychedelic white and blue flowered background. Then the egg is gone and there is centerfold sugar gleaming white on white. Languid oil follows sugar and then salt takes its turn, lounging in the square bowl. It looks like a pop-art pictorial on how to make pancakes.

Sabiha doesn't know the website *Al-Zawra* so she puts some text into Google Translator. "For women who are interested in explosive belt and suicide bombing—"

Right now, Sabiha wishes she were under her quilted bedspread listening to Lana Del Rey on her headphones. Then she wouldn't have to think about Hiba's head, arms and legs blasting off her body like the rays off a starfish. She wouldn't hear the whirl of helicopters harmonizing with a chorus of sirens. Goosebumps flower her back.

She should tell someone. What if someone already knows? What if the NSA is watching her right now through the library computer? Wait, there's no camera on the monitor. For safety, Sabiha ties Hiba's *kaffiyeh* around her face, gangsta style. The soft cloth smells of sweat and rose water.

The Sisterhood of the Caliphate shows girls about Sabiha's age carrying AK-47s, teens decorated with grenades. One poster child wears a stethoscope around her neck and a Kalashnikov on her shoulder. There are classes in cooking and sewing and weaponry. The Sisterhood gather like the suburban moms in Rockridge do, minding their kids together on playgrounds. But all work and no play makes Jill a very cranky *hausfrau*. These *jihadi* wives meet for coffee or go to restaurants backlit by sunsets while they wait for their handsome husbands to be martyred in the holy war.

Sabiha twirls a lock of her hair instead of chewing it. The girls in the photos are part of something bigger. They matter. At school, the only girls that matter are the cheerleaders and the half-sluts, and there's a lot of overlap. Jesse would never write on her with his fountain pen ink eyes. His hard/soft mouth would never inch in her direction. She sees herself as her classmates see her, a loner, the dull cream school walls surrounding her like a milk carton. What did Hiba call them? Sand niggers? Sabiha has never thought of herself like a—there's no polite way to say it—sand nigger. But, Hiba's right. Even Sabiha's father doesn't give her the time of day. She gathers her things and exits the computer room, lingering in the doorway like a climbing vine. Her face wears a complicated look full of gratitude and grief, inferiority and anger, all at the same time. Outside, twilight aches amethyst.

Sabiha boards the bus with Hiba's *kaffiyeh* hugging her shoulders. Someone's body odor isn't taking no for an answer. The plastic seat freezes the bejeezus beneath her skirt. She misses her jeans, abandoned in her locker. The bus passes Oscar Grant Plaza, which is empty. In her head, Sabiha hears the throaty unhappiness of an oboe.

The bus rolls to a stop, miles before the intersection. A sea of brown, pin pricked by ovals of white, pools at the center of the traffic lights. It's a giant sleepover under a gray lid of clouds. The Black Lives Matter protestors have staged a die-in to plague the evening rush hour.

Sabiha watches her hand receive a signal from somewhere she does not care and press the Stop Requested button. Her body leads. Her feet keep time to a quick percussion like congas being played in a park until she is halfway down the block. Her brain follows. At the perimeter of the die-in, dead silence coats the reclining bodies. There's a sizzle in the air that Sabiha recognizes as possibility. She walks the dotted-line map of feet meeting heads until space enough for her opens on the ground. As she lies down, she's sure she's on the verge of pleasure. This shimmering feeling is invisible and everywhere. The people on either side of her take her hands.

"Thanks for coming out." The words are beaded together. After all, the protestors are supposed to be dead.

"Of course. No problem." Sabiha wears a new face.

"It's cool having one of you support one of us. Peace."

Sabiha feels her skin sprout steel scales. When she speaks, her voice has a caramel edge. "Muslim lives matter too." Her neighbor grasps her hand tighter. His fingers are warmly moist and slightly disgustingly cozy.

From nowhere, a necklace of floating diamonds encircles the die-in. Waves of sound rush the protestors: rocks spanking concrete, glass shattering into teardrops, a stampede of cops moving in. The hands holding Sabiha's play a tug-of-war as they pull her up. Her eyes stream. The air tastes like bitter fire, and it's getting hard to breathe.

"Wait! My backpack!" In her bag, the Rehana photo beats like a heart. Sabiha wishbones her right hand free to retrieve her bag and stumbles in the process. A lone shot cracks the air.

Cocooning her bag, she's lifted up by a tide of people running. Sabiha runs too, and in her mind the dry Oakland asphalt sprouts lush green grass and slants uphill. She is running with Rehana, running with the Kurds, running with the mountains into safety. The icy pitch of syncopated piano keys scores her retreat.

The protestors scatter like lab mice freed into a world they can't wait to explore. Sabiha smiles a private smile as she runs—she can't help smiling—this is the most alive she has ever felt. Now she understands why the Al-Zawra website instructs girls to train every day. Protest is hard work. She wonders if she should give up Kit-Kats.

Up ahead, a boy and girl, running and still holding hands, disappear into the seam of two buildings. Sabiha follows as much from lack of choice as from curiosity. There is an alley, nearly invisible from the street. Inside its trellised entrance, leaves glitter as they shiver. Sabiha doesn't feel the cold yet; sweat spiders her eyebrows. Somewhere, a siren screeches.

"Hey." The girl's whisper stretches from a cartwheel of grass in the back corner.

"Hi. I followed you." Sabiha's tongue hangs like a wilted flag.

"No problem. No one wants to get caught." The boy has eyes of polished blue stone.

"Yeah. What happens if you do?"

"First protest?" The girl coos like Sabiha is a child. "No, it's all good. Better to start some time than no time. This is our seventh. We met at Occupy Oakland."

Sabiha thinks about the Sisterhood working alongside their husbands. "That's really romantic."

Blue Eyes focuses on some distant place where protest is a religion. "The cops usually just arrest you and bring you down to central booking. Sooner or later you get to go home."

The word pumpkins her. "Shit," Sabiha the Protestor swears. "I need to go." She adds her sweat to the *kaffiyeh* before stuffing it in the bottom of her bag. "Can you point me towards 27th and Telegraph Avenue please?"

Sirood is waiting for her at the door. He stands too close, inhaling sharply. Sabiha pushes past him.

"What gives?" Sabiha sniffs herself. Underneath her girl smell is the scent of independence blossoming. She is a peony spreading its petals.

"Have you been smoking?"

"What? No!" Sabiha burps into Sirood's face. It is a throwback to when she was a kid and would lean in to tell a secret but burp instead. "See?"

A faint smile flirts with the corners of Sirood's mouth. "Okay, I believe you."

That burp works every time.

"I was worried. Why so late?"

Sabiha parks her hand on Sirood's shoulder as she peels off her shoes. "There was a die-in during rush hour. The buses couldn't get through."

"I saw it on TV."

"I finally got off and walked." Which is only a half lie. Which is why Sabiha feels only half guilty.

Sirood gets lost in a moment, "Sorry, you looked just like Mom for a second. Listen, next time stay on the bus. It's safer than the street. Someone might think you're a protestor. You could get arrested."

Sabiha tunes out Sirood to hear the hum of things: the television murmuring in the living room and the buzz of the light bulbs illuminating the hallway. She chews the insides of her cheeks to keep from saying *So?* and sends her softest voice out from between her lips. "You're right. Next time I'll be more careful." Why did it take so long to realize how easy this is? People want to hear what they want to hear. This adult thing is so simple. Sabiha sees an older version of herself slung diagonally across an armchair.

Sirood goes into the kitchen. "Mom went to the gym. I can heat some leftovers. How does that sound?"

Sabiha's so hungry that leftovers make her feel lucky. She answers over the kiss of the fridge. "Yeah, sounds great." She doesn't care if those leftovers were being made as Sirood talked to their father.

Later, in the shower, where her thoughts are always honest, Sabiha confronts the day's events. Turning the water hotter doesn't erase that horrible knowing feeling, even as her flesh scalds. She lets the water pour. It is a voice washing over her: big-throated and primitive, alive like a heart.

Lavender light filters through the library window, hazing the computer room. It's been five days and twenty-three hours since Sabiha found Shams' blog, *Diary of a Caliphette,* on Tumblr and five days and twenty-one hours since Shams friended Sabiha on Facebook.

Thurs 3:47 PM

OMG. Sabiha, have you tried those peanut butter Kit-Kats? Way better than white. ☺

The white Twix is better than the Kat.

I'll have to try. Bring some if you come. You'll die over this new liner I got. My sister brought it back from Gaziantep. They have more choice than here. It's like five thousand times more silky. Ooooooooh She brought pistachios too ☺. I am gonna get fat.

LOL. Hardly. I'm sure working at the hospital keeps you skinny.

I love what I'm doing now. There are too many broken kids, thanks to ASS-ad. This war is heartbreaking. I'm glad I made *hijra*.

I could never.

Sure you could, if you want. That *ask. fm* website tells you how to get here and join jihad. It's easier than you think. Most things in life usually are. Just get to Turkey. From there, Syria is a snap.

This girl is so cool! Sabiha flicks through Shams' photos on Facebook while they message back and forth. Envy bites her insides. Shams is *living*! Sabiha wishes they could Skype. She bets the music of Shams' voice is bold and triumphant, like Metallica covered by the San Francisco Symphony.

Anyway, let's finish this quiz. Don't you want to know which of the Prophet's wives you're most like?

I hope I'm an Aisha. ☺

I'm a Maryam. ☺

Everyone wants to be a Maryam. She bore the Prophet's son, she could sing, she was gorgeous. But Aisha had fire. She was a warrior. She did things.

OK, *SabAisha*. Number 6: What is your preferred hairstyle? A) Pinned loosely to your head; B) Cascading down your shoulders; C) However my husband prefers it.

I like Rehana's braid.

She's a Kurd. They fight against us. I'm glad one of our holy warriors beheaded her.

Sabiha?

Are you there?

Sabibti?

????????

Cascading down my shoulders.

Number 7: If you were an animal, what kind of animal would you be? A) Lion; B) Falcon; C) Kitten.

Falcon

What is your weapon of choice? A) AK-47; B) Knife; C) Suicide vest/explosives.

Ugh. None of the above.

Not a choice. You wouldn't say that if you saw what the world is doing to us over here. It's trying to make being alive unbearable. I'm going to send you some pics.

AK-47?

How can you best serve the new Islamic Utopia? A) Doctor; B) Soldier, C) Child Bearer.

Soldier

Right. You can't even pick a weapon. I'm marking Child Bearer. Okay, last one: Describe your ideal Prince Charming:
A) Tall, dark and bearded;
B) Short, dark and bearded;
C) Whomever Allah sees fit.

Really???!!!

What "Really"?

C

Of course, C. Okay, you have a score of 17. You're a Zaynab, which is almost as good as an Aisha. She stood by Aisha when all of Medina turned against her. Loyalty rocks. Plus, she made like totally beautiful handicrafts and sold them to benefit the household and gave money to the poor. You'll have no prob finding a husband.

Do you like being married?

Yeah! My life has meaning. I support my husband in building a new society where everyone matters. I'm part of it. Plus, it's fun trying to make babies. ☺

I could never marry someone I didn't know.

I could introduce you to a few warriors on FB. You could chat and get to know each other the right way. You learn the real person, the inside, instead of thinking you love someone because he looks like that judge on *Arab Idol*.

Or Channing Tatum.
I love him. ♥

 Me too. We could find you your
very own right here. ♥

I dunno.

 Think about it. You really need to get a
smart phone. Listen, I have to go to the
hospital. Sending a few pics now. Bye
SabAisha.

Thanks Shams. Bye. ☺

A piano note heralds the arrival of photo attachments. The first one is a makeshift ward of melted, bloody children who were gassed by Assad. They died open-mouthed, like baby birds.

Sabiha stares at the photo until her heart bangs against the bars. It's the kind of photo that doesn't let you shirk responsibility. And Shams lives it, works it, strives to stop it.

The next photo is a smiling fighter holding up a woman's severed head. A long blond braid trails past the floating orb like a kite tail. Janis Joplin screeches raw violet in Sabiha's inner ear. Her stomach swoops to her mouth as she chokes back a bit of puke. She puts her hands to her own neck, resting them on her butter knife collar bones until her stomach calms. She gets Rehana's V photo from her backpack and holds it to the computer screen. V

Rehana has open eyes, a butterscotch face, and a neck propping up her head. Dead Rehana has closed eyes, a white face, and bloody lacey edges where a neck should be. The smiling fighter has a body, neck, and head, topped with a backwards baseball cap. The smiling fighter and V Rehana wage a staring contest. Sabiha opens Google and V Rehana wins.

According to *MailOnLine*, Rehana, alive and well, escaped to southern Turkey. Sabiha sees her running under a blueberry sherbet sky, running over soil that is less like cookie dough and more like cookie crumbs as she crosses the border, her defiant, streaming braid the color of a lemon wheel when you hold it to the sun. Full of gratitude, Sabiha's heart beats a chocolatey dum-tee-dum.

How could Shams have gotten it so wrong? Sabiha's heart hardens to a peach pit. A pinwheel in her mind rotates the faces of everyone who confuses her: Shams, Sirood, Jesse and his nipple-grazed girlfriend, her father. In that moment she hates them all, which really means she hates herself. She wishes she were in the pink cocoon of her bedroom, so she could fling herself onto her bubble gum bed and bite her pillow. In her mind's eye, Sabiha breathes in colors, soft rose and thistle, until the self-loathing she cannot name subsides and her eyelashes no longer gleam. She shuts down the computer. Her reflection in the computer screen taunts her, like it wants to get her into trouble. Sabiha diverts her gaze through the window, to the stained-glass sky.

Outside the cool air kisses her face. Sabiha hears the wedding dress elegance of harp music as she approaches the bus stop. Across the street, a busker, all elbows and sharp angles, cradles the wooden frame, plucking at its strings. The delicate notes whirl across the street and pull Sabiha towards them. She laces through the crowd until she's close enough to feel the vibrations electrify each follicle of arm hair. When the harpist finishes playing, Sabiha roots inside her jacket pocket for some change. She has lost her taste for Kit Kats.

"Thanks." The harpist's voice is as milky as her skin.

Sabiha wants to pluck the strings, to create the petal-soft music of dawn breaking with her own fingertips. She waits expectantly. The harpist resumes playing, not sparing another glance in Sabiha's direction. The size of the crowd ebbs and flows. As darkness cleaves to the streetlights, Sabiha jams her hands into her empty pockets and ambles towards the bus stop in her own private silence, slowly home.

Kurdistan

I AM FIFTEEN YEARS OLD. MY PARENTS ARE DEAD. I have a blue bird puppet named Annie made out of that fake fur they use for fuzzy pencils in my carry-on bag, and a copy of *To Kill a Mockingbird* in my lap. The heavyset woman next to me keeps offering me Oreo cookies from the pointy black purse balanced on her belly. There is chocolate dust around the corners of her mouth but I don't have the nerve to tell her. Instead, I look out the window of the plane and see a shadow girl staring back at me.

I am moving to Kurdistan. Most Americans think Kurdistan is Kyrgyzstan unless they are from Nashville or San Diego where a lot of Kurdish people live. Those people know Kurdistan is in northern Iraq. They know it has mountains. And green parts. And oil.

Aunt Maya is waiting for me outside the security checkpoint. Her blue headscarf is bedazzled. Red hair peeks out from the sides. She hugs me the same way Mom used to—hands pressing both sides of my face—and asks if I remember her. Through squeezed cheeks I pucker yes and breathe in Shalimar. I want to take Annie out of my carry-on, but I know I am too old to play with her in public.

This part of Kurdistan doesn't look green. It's brown and dusty. Aunt Maya leads me to a gleaming white Land Cruiser. I wonder how she keeps the dust off. Her driver takes my bags. He wears mirrored sunglasses and a dark suit with a dark tie. Aunt Maya and I sit in the back. The car smells like her perfume and new plastic. There is an odd-looking rifle poking up from the floor of the front seat.

The highway leading from the airport is dotted with parked cars. Whole families with mothers and fathers and daughters picnic at the side of the road. Women in long colorful dresses sit on brown grass around open fires. The men wear what look like a brown onesie belted with a wide sash. They remind me of feet pajamas. As we drive, a fiery sun sinks down and divides the sky into a band of blue squashing a band of orange to conquer the horizon. We pass clusters of identical new homes that look like they have been cut from raw cookie dough. There is a mall with amusement park rides. A roller coaster towers behind a sign announcing Family Land.

Aunt Maya asks, You have Family Land in Tennessee?

It takes me a moment to figure out what she means. Then I see her looking at the sign. I tell her we have malls, but not with roller coasters.

She says, I take you.

It is hilly and my ears haven't adjusted from the plane. I squeeze my nose and exhale. It doesn't work. Every sound comes to me from underwater. We pass a gated compound with orange buildings. There are soldiers at the entrance with the same odd-looking rifles as the driver has. In front of the gate is a collapsible grate with jagged metal teeth. Aunt Maya points and tells me that is my new school.

We pass a big fancy hotel on a hill across from a field where sheep are grazing. Fuzzy gray bleeds into fuzzy white. We turn right into a compound called American Village. All the houses are big-big. Uniformed guards circle the car, sticking long, shiny mirrored shovels under it. I don't know what they are looking for. We pass inspection and enter. We pull up to a cookie-dough mansion with white Grecian pillars. The garage juts outward onto the front lawn. Aunt Maya squeezes my arm. We're home.

Around the side of the house the backyard unfolds into a patio palace. A marble dance floor holds court between an outdoor fireplace made of the same marble-y stone and a high-tech DJ station. Adjacent to the fireplace is a sitting area with thick-cushioned couches and a full bar. Our old apartment would fit onto half the patio.

Aunt Maya sees me staring and asks if I'm OK. Her big eyes shine like glass. I don't have the right words so I smile with closed lips. My smile forms a tight line. I tight-line smile a lot these days. The right words don't exist. I would need to invent a whole new language.

Both died in cars. Back home in Tennessee, Mom was at an intersection by a mosque when a bomb went off. She wasn't wearing her seat belt. Dad was an interpreter for the US Army in Iraq, and he died when his car drove over an IED. He was wearing a seat belt. What are the chances?

Chance is like one of those black scorpions that blindly stings anything that gets in its path. Mom got stung last month. Dad got stung eight years ago.

Mom and Dad were the only ones in their families to emigrate to the US when Saddam was killing Kurds. Now they are gone and Saddam is gone, so the lawyers thought I should go there, here, to be with family. All my relatives are here. Aunt Maya is Mom's sister and she was married to a government minister and that's probably why her house is so big.

Inside it's like a museum. There are paintings behind thick glass in gold curlicue frames. The porcelain tiles feel cold under my bare feet. Aunt Maya leads me past a woman stuffing meat and rice into hollowed peppers in the kitchen, upstairs to a bedroom, and all I think is I'm going to get lost in this house. French doors open onto a pink and white room with thick plush carpet. The room smells like almonds and fresh paint. My two oversized suitcases are huddled in the corner. From the doorway, I see their frayed edges. Hopefully, Aunt Maya doesn't see them too. On the dresser is a cloth framed photograph of two girls in long water-colored gowns. Rhinestones dance down their dress fronts and jitterbug onto their *hijabs*. Red hair peeks out from the sides of their head scarves.

I picture Mom in her skinny jeans jumping up to play air guitar whenever her favorite songs were on the radio. Then I see her in a vintage rock T-shirt drinking milk out of the carton when she thought no one was looking. I have never seen her wear a head scarf.

As soon as Aunt Maya leaves, Annie comes out of my carry-on. She's smushed from being packed for so long. With my hand inside her yellow felt beak, she comes to life. Holding her close, I inhale her dusty synthetic odor. She tells me to let her go so she can investigate the room. I make Annie kiss me and feel the cold metal of her beak ring against my lip. Mom pierced her beak to show me it didn't hurt before I got my ears pierced on my tenth birthday.

Inside the walk-in closet, a row of empty hangers confronts Annie and me. We fall down under them. I have been steam rolled. All the air leaves my chest and I can't swallow. The carpet itches my cheek but I can't scratch it. I can't move. I stare directly into Annie's crossed eyes until I become cross-eyed too. We are both two dimensional. Putting all my concentration into breathing, I will my lungs to beat like a bird's wings flapping. Gradually, I puff myself back into shape.

~

At 5:02, the call to prayer breaks the morning silence. The plaintive sound reminds me of a coffee commercial. Dusty brown hills meet the low-hanging sky outside my bedroom window. All the colors are washed out in the filmy air. Somewhere, a rooster crows.

My stomach growls, but I am too chicken to go to the kitchen and help myself. Annie finally dares me into action. I tiptoe down the stairs, take a wrong turn, and end up in the library. The books look old. All the titles are in Kurdish. I make out only a few words. Some have Aunt Maya's surname running along the sides. Outside the library window, the driver is washing Aunt Maya's car. Long, bumpy scars the color of bacon fat crisscross the back of his upper arms and shoulders, disappearing beneath his sleeveless tee. The woman who was preparing food yesterday brings him a mug. Her hand lingers on his forearm. Watching her retrace her steps helps me find my way to the kitchen.

She is making smoothies and doesn't hear me above the whirl of the blender. She uses her right shoulder to itch her cheek without breaking her smoothie-making stride. She has a blister-size mole on the side of her cheek and I wonder if her shoulder feels it. There are lines pulling down the corners of her mouth. She could be anywhere from thirty to fifty. She turns and is startled. She points to the blender and says something in Kurdish. I nod my head, and she hands me a glass. She smells like a just-opened can of Campbell's Chicken Noodle soup.

She looks at me and waits. I don't know what I am supposed to do. I want to take the smoothie and run back to my room, but I don't want to be rude. I finish it in one gulp and walk my glass over to the sink. She fires out something in Kurdish and grabs for the glass. Maybe she doesn't want me to wash it out. I tell her it's OK, I don't mind. She is surprisingly strong and won't let go of it. Together, we carry the glass to the sink. I don't dare rinse it.

She nods at the kitchen table and smiles. I nod at the kitchen table and smile back. She hands me a mug of steaming black tea and pushes me towards the table. I finally remember the Kurdish for thank you, which sounds like *zor spas*. A flurry of plates appears. The honey is lighter than back home, the bread is darker. There is creamy goat's cheese and giant, juicy burgundy red grapes. She spoons fresh pomegranate seeds onto my plate from a large bowl. There is so much color. I take a tiny bite of cheese dipped in honey but it won't go down. Aunt Maya walks in as I start to cough and hands me a glass of water. She keeps her hand on my back as I drink, which makes drinking it even harder.

You meet Trahzia? Upon hearing her name, the woman washing dishes turns around and smiles. She is missing a side tooth.

I did, Aunt Maya.

Trahzia bring you anything what you want, Aunt Maya reassures.

Holding my breath, I meet Aunt Maya's gaze. My right eye twitches.

Aunt Maya strokes my hair and says Today we go shopping, and getting you ready for the school. Later we ride a—here she makes a loop-de-loop motion with her hand—sound good? You shower and we go to the Family Land.

~~

You want to know? How I do it? How I keep my ache silent? How I can go shopping or ride roller coasters while Mom is in a sunless box under brown earth, and Dad is blowing across the desert? Thinking about it starts The Pit of Loneliness twisting in my gut and makes me want to stay under the hot shower until every bit of me melts down the drain.

Aunt Maya sits down so close I see the tiny hairs standing up on her neck. You talk about it Shatu?

No thanks.

Talking help, no? Aunt Maya asks.

No. No. It doesn't.

Aunt Maya has two sons, but they go to school in the UK. She started painting when the younger went abroad. Aunt Maya's paintings are like nothing I've seen in Nashville. She re- creates moments in Kurdish history on series of old wooden doors set in manufactured pathways of broken glass and rubble. She laughs without smiling when she tells me of breaking sheets of new glass and slabs of stone to make fake destroyed villages. Aunt Maya shows me some pictures of an installation she did for a museum in Halabja. The painted people look really creepy. Lots of melting noses, huge lifeless eyes, wide-open screaming mouths. Sometimes she attaches found objects so the paintings become like sculptures. There is one door with a charred stuffed animal dangling from a painted little girl's burnt hand. Aunt Maya's studio is housed in a cultural center that sometimes shows her work. She says the people who should see her work don't go to cultural centers.

On Saturday morning she goes to her studio, so I'm left alone with Trahzia. By noon, I have unpacked my suitcases and filled the empty hangers in my closet. The starched white school uniform shirts look like they belong to someone else. Restless, I head to the library.

Ignoring the uh-oh feeling, I sit at Aunt Maya's desk and pull open a drawer that looks promising. Inside are wrinkled newspaper clippings detailing Uncle Mazen's death in 2004 when suicide bombers blew up the Kurdistan

Democratic Party office and the Patriotic Union of Kurdistan office at the same time. Uncle Mazen was Aunt Maya's husband. Mom didn't come back for the funeral which was right after Dad's. For the first time I wonder if she regretted it.

There is a Kurdish flag wrapped around a military medal and a silver-framed, old-fashioned photograph of Uncle Mazen with the current Kurdish President standing close to a young woman who looks an awful lot like Aunt Maya. I feel like a kid with her hand in the cookie jar when Trahzia comes in to dust.

She leans over me, putting everything back into the drawer and gurgles something in singsong Kurdish. Then she pulls me up by the arm and leads me through the first floor to the part of the house where she lives with the driver. The insides of their rooms pulse with color. A massive orange and pink kiln dominates their sitting room. Cushions of every size and shade of red are thrown helter-skelter around a low copper table. Green plants snake along the walls. There is so much life in the peaceful stillness of the space.

Trahzia seats me on a cushion near the window and lays my head back. She passes her hands over my eyes to close them. They smell like vanilla cake batter. Suddenly, something vibrates along my eyebrows. It sounds like a fingernail running along plastic comb teeth. I cock one eye open and watch two threads crisscross along my brow bone and disappear between Trahzia's teeth. A bead of saliva threatens the corner of her mouth.

She surveys her work with satisfaction and hands me a mirror. For a moment I don't recognize myself. The eyes that peer back at me seem bigger and somehow brighter. They look like Mom's eyes.

The sun glints off the mirror creating a spotlight and that's when I see it behind one of the winding vines. A photo of three young girls, two with red hair, dressed in traditional clothing, performing a dance. The third girl is missing a side tooth. My face pivots towards the photograph. *Chopy,* says Trahzia pointing at the picture. *Chopy,* says Trahzia as she takes my hand and pulls me up. *Chopy,* says Trahzia as she bounces from left foot to right foot travelling across the floor. I stand like a statue. I have never seen this dance.

Trahzia is determined to teach me the *chopy* steps. Left foot out. Were Mom and Trahzia and Aunt Maya all friends when they were kids? Right foot out. Why does Trahzia work for Aunt Maya? Cross left. Were they part of a dance troupe? Step right. Why is the President in an old picture with Mom? Left back. Where was Dad during all this? Left foot out. Are there more photos?

I point to the photograph and ask Trahzia for more. She starts to dance again. I shake my head no and point to the picture again. Trahzia lifts her shoulders. I mime taking a picture and she disappears behind a closed door. My body tightens and wants to throw itself among the crimson cushions, kicking and screaming. Trahzia returns holding a worn brown leather book.

The inside pages smell of cedar. The beginning photos are all of Mom, Aunt Maya, and Trahzia when they were young. Here they are picnicking with family outside an ancient monastery carved into a hillside. Here they are in their dancing costumes at a family wedding by a lake. Here they are in school uniforms, Trahzia mugging for the camera, Mom wearing a hijab.

Trahzia wordlessly stops my hand from turning the page and looks at me with such seriousness that I am back in our kitchen in Nashville about to find out that Mom will never again make me macaroni and cheese with bread crumbs on top because she is never coming home. A sweat bead trickles down my armpit. The next page shows photos of homemade tents set against a backdrop of snow-capped mountains. There are too many people for the number of tents, all looking hungry and tired. A red-haired, dirty-faced teenager stares murderously while her hijab-wearing sister sits with her chin sunk onto her chest. Looking at the photos makes me feel like I'm lying under a slab of lead and maybe it would be better never to get up.

I stare at the hardened eyes captured in the photograph of Mom's face. My mom—my cartoon-voice-inventing, bed-sheet-fort-on-a-school-night-making, Meals-on-Wheels-delivering, Kurdish-immigrant, dead-from-a-hit-and-run-driver-fleeing-a-bomb-explosion-outside-a-mosque mom—looks like she could kill someone. Looking at Mom's eyes in that picture sends all my blood to my toes.

Anfal, Trahzia says, and goes catatonic. Then she shakes herself like a dog after a jump in a pond, snaps the album shut, and puts it somewhere only snooping will find.

Anfal?

I know about *Anfal.* Every Kurd knows at least the Wikipedia minimum. I didn't know Mom had actually lived it. What else don't I know? Aunt Maya comes home at 5:37.

Aunt Maya, I say, you're right. Talking might help.

Aunt Maya smiles, takes off her hijab, and sits down at the kitchen table. She pats the seat next to her.

I don't sit down. How long were you in the camps? What happened to Mom in the camps? Why did she stop wearing the hijab? Why is there a picture of Mom with the President? Where was Dad during all this?

Aunt Maya's head and shoulders slump as she bunches the headscarf on the table into a crumpled ball. She looks like the last plastic doll left on a K-Mart shelf at Christmas time. For about thirty seconds we both listen to air.

Anfal. The word escapes her mouth more than she says it. She goes into the library and returns with one of the books that has her surname on it. She tells me Uncle Mazen wrote about the eighth and final phase of *Anfal* in the Barzan heartland where Saddam killed Kurdistan Democratic Party families and demolished countless villages. Inside there are more pictures of destroyed villages and makeshift mountain camps.

You and Mom and Trahzia are from a Barzan village? Aunt Maya nods her head.

I wonder if I am related to the President.

Trahzia puts out platters of food which no one eats. The firm basmati rice of the *biryani* sits in perfect mounds, bits of chicken and plump sultana peeping out. Chunks of eggplant, zucchini, peppers, and potatoes wait patiently in rich ripe tomato sauce for spoons that never come. There are side salads of green, purple, and orange to fill out the table. At home we used to have one main dish and one salad that we would share.

Trahzia still won't let me help clear the table. Aunt Maya asks, How much tell you your mom the camps?

Some, I lie.

Aunt Maya leads me out onto the patio where we sit next to each other on a cushiony wicker loveseat. It seems strange to sit on living room furniture outside. The sun looks like a giant butterscotch candy coating the sky. Aunt Maya and I stare at it and listen to the zhur-zhur- zhur of lawn sprinklers as we both wait for her to begin.

There was whispers of marching and killing men. Our men going to mountains for training and fighting. Some men stay in village to protection. Saddam men come. We no see our men again. Saddam men do bad things. We womans running to mountains. Many Kurdish peoples running to mountains.

Aunt Maya is breathing heavily and stops speaking for many moments. A chorus of insects fills the silence followed by the bleating call to prayer. Nearby, someone is grilling chicken shish.

Your mom very beautiful, is what she says next.

Was Aunt Maya. Yes she was. My voice is so quiet I wonder if she hears me.

Bad mans doing bad thing to beautiful womans.

An olive-green lizard darts across the marble-y stone and melds into the drab, dry grass.

Woman losing honor. Family losing honor. Important village man don't married woman with no honor. Woman must to marry or… or, or must to… be no more for family having honor. Elders…say…in camp…mom no more for bringing back family honor. Your father hear and he steal her to America.

I remember the picture I found in Aunt Maya's desk. Did Mom and Dad love each other?

There different kind of love. Your father loving Dilin since they small. Your mom grateful he to marry to her and safe her. She loving him later. Life has long, Aunt Maya says as she tries to put her arm around me.

I am not a hugger.

All night the thought's tentacles nip at the collar of my T-shirt, pin me in place, and choke me at the same time. If it happens eventually, why not do it now? Then at least The Pit of Loneliness wouldn't take root inside my stomach and hollow me from inside out. Mom and I could be together. I have already lost the smell of her. Annie spends the night on my pillow instead of on her shelf.

Trahzia, Aunt Maya says, joined the *Pesh Merga* after her father and brothers were tortured and killed by the Ba'ath party in an underground prison. She fought with the Barzani tribe for the Kurdistan Democratic Party against Saddam during *Anfal* and against the Barzani tribe in the mid-1990s when the Barzanis teamed up with Saddam against the Patriotic Union of Kurdistan. It's hard to picture those same hands which fold flaky filo dough around nuts and honey holding one of those funny-looking rifles Aunt Maya's driver keeps in the car.

Now that Saddam is dead, Trahzia is no longer a soldier. Instead, she seems happy to wield a knife against a pile of multi-colored fruit or stuff rice and meat into vegetables.

Sometimes I watch and we trade words as she cooks. She points to a fig she's chopping and says *hajir*. I point back and say fig. Then she gives me a piece. I say *hajir* over and over again inside my head until I have swallowed. I don't know what she says inside her head as she chews. Sometimes she just stands real still and closes her eyes.

~

I have been in Kurdistan for nine days when Lila calls me on Skype. Lila is a drummer in a surf rockabilly band and can't sleep with anything covering her feet. She lives across the hall from our old apartment in Nashville and used to babysit me when I was a little kid. It's 2:57 back home. Lila must have just finished a gig because her makeup looks runny. She asks how I'm doing. Hearing her gravelly southern twang cocoons me in Nashville hominess: the soft worn of a grandmother-crocheted Afghan blanket covering your shoulders, honky-tonk music drifting up from hidden courtyards, fireflies illuminating birch leaves, streetlights lending playing children an extra hour. And somehow in that buttered-toast scent of normal life, Lila sits at her laptop computer with a hand-rolled cigarette burning at her side to ask an orphan in Kurdistan how she is doing.

Lila sees my tight-line smile on her computer screen and tells me to breathe.

I ask her if she had a gig.

She says she did. It was a benefit for Mom and she wants to know which charity to send the money to in Mom's name. She knows the mosque needs money to rebuild. Do I want to send it there? Thinking about what happened to Mom in the camps makes me tell her to send it to Meals on Wheels and that I have to go.

She says she misses me. A new family has moved into our apartment and it just isn't the same. She takes a drag on her cigarette and blows me a smoke ring kiss, and with my one keystroke she is gone.

Some other mother and daughter are going to sit on our peanut curry spotted sofa cushions to play checkers. They are going to make Aqua Fresh toothpaste mustaches sharing one sink in our black and white bathroom. They'll drink honey ginger tea from the footed teacups Mom bought at a yard sale. They'll swing our old pillows that leak feathers in epic pillow fights on Sunday mornings. They'll use everything, all of our junk, and their spirits will push out our ghosts and someday not even Lila will miss us. And I'm living in luxury, and I've got all these memories but not the person who created them. I am seven thousand miles and five weeks away and every minute is a moment without the one person who made the world make sense. And I'm supposed to live with Aunt Maya in Kurdistan for like what, the rest of my life?

Thinking about some other mom helping her daughter with math homework at our wobbly kitchen table wakes the Pit of Loneliness inside my chest. The Pit stretches, its spiky circular blades whirling away my insides so all that is left is an empty husk. Falling back on my bed, the sound of the ocean rushes into my ears and I am drowning in muddy gray murkiness. I sink past Dad in his marine greens holding a bouquet of flowers in one hand and a one hundred and twenty count Crayola Crayon box in the other. I sink past Mom smothering slices of green apple in chunky peanut butter as she devours *Entertainment Weekly*. I sink past Boo Radley tip toeing across a lawn to leave small presents in the hollow of a tree before running home and slamming his wooden trap door tightly shut.

The smell of baking cookies steals under my bedroom door. I smell the neighbor's sun-scorched freshly cut grass, and the desert's far-flung roasted sand, and the sharp animal scent of grazing sheep. Multi-colored pinpoints rain beneath my eyelids. Trahzia enters my room. Scents of cinnamon, cardamom, and coffee saunter in behind her. A drop of water slides down my cheek. She says something in swishy-slushy Kurdish and pulls me from the bed to the window which she closes. A fog of milky dust whips from the sky over the marble-y tiles and lawn.

Shamal, Trahzia says with admiration.

I don't know if *shamal* means dust or sand or wind, but whatever it is, it is pretty cool. It has power and awe and I want to swallow it whole into the Pit of Loneliness. I picture the *shamal* breaking the Pit's huge mechanical jaw hinges, grinding the Pit to a halt. As Trahzia and I wordlessly watch the storm bend and break young sapling trees and menace our window panes, and my insides slowly fill back in, I swear, I see an old man in a long white robe walk out of the center of the storm. The man has a white flowing beard and porcelain white bare feet and he carries what look like prayer beads and he rights the broken-back trees and turns and roars at the storm. Then he is absorbed into its center and disappears.

The wind completely dies just as suddenly as it started. Trahzia opens the window. The air smells sweet like cucumbers. The streets are absolutely silent. The trees have healed themselves upright.

Did you see him? I know you saw him. Look at that tree, I say pointing to a now-healthy young sapling.

Trahzia whispers what sounds like Mar Yosip and continues from room to room opening windows. I open Google.

Aunt Maya gets home at 6:03.

Aunt Maya, I say. I want to go to church.

Mom never talked about religion. The religion she grew up with said she was bad because someone did something bad to her even though she was following the rules. That doesn't seem fair. Aunt Maya says it's about culture too. Honor and purity are part of both Islam and being Kurdish, and I shouldn't turn my back on either, and would I like to try the hijab? The look on my face stops her argument mid-sentence. In the end, she buys me a modest long-sleeved navy-blue dress with a round collar and sends me to the nearby Christian city of Ankawa with the driver.

The Christians in Ankawa are mostly Assyrian if you don't count the expats. Mar Yosip is the official saint of the Assyrian Church and is known for his gifts of mysticism and healing. Figuring a saint wouldn't seek the limelight, I head to Saint George's Assyrian Church because it is small and cozy. Aunt Maya says Mar Yosip is a long dead archbishop, not a saint that appears during sandstorms to repair broken trees and I shouldn't expect to find him in a pew praying. I point out that Trahzia said his name so she must have seen him too. Aunt Maya scowls at this and reminds me that lots of people refer to Santa Claus, but that doesn't mean he slides down their chimneys. This makes me smile because I don't expect Aunt Maya in her diamante hijab to argue a point using Santa Claus.

I am surprised when a round-bellied guard stops me at the church courtyard entrance to ask me if I am a Christian. I lie uncertainly, causing him to half-heartedly search my bag. I wonder who is watching us. Gravel paths snake around the vast courtyard behind guard posts and plots of needle-y grass before leading to the church's unadorned entrance.

The church seems much smaller from inside. Men sit on one side while women sit on the other. Most of the older women wear lace cloths on top of their heads. Some of the lace head coverings match one another like high school team jackets. The service is in Assyrian, so I understand nothing. There is chanting and incense burning and a procession around the pews. The priest carries a gold-covered Bible that some of the men kiss and the women gently pat before blessing themselves. And then it is over.

I am the last person to leave the church. I kick gravel from the paths as I stomp over to the car. The guard eyeballs me. I saw Mar Yosip. I saw him mend trees. I saw him quiet the storm. But inside his church, I felt nothing. No wonder Aunt Maya doesn't believe me. But if I didn't see Mar Yosip heal trees and calm a storm, how can I ever hope to fill the Pit of Loneliness? Its wrecking jaws scrape to life as I approach the car. I slam my car door startling the driver. The raw ache that is my insides swells until I am doubled over in the back seat. It is several minutes before I realize we are headed in the opposite direction of Aunt Maya's house.

Heading west past the airport, there is nothing but vast, empty land. We wind silently through the rugged reddish-brown foothills of Saffine Mountain until the driver pulls onto a chalky brown shoulder halfway hidden in a sun shadow. I hear a crescendoing popping noise that reminds me of exploding popcorn cooked old-school in a pot over a stove top. As I lift my head, Trahzia swaggers out from behind a small scab-colored ridge swinging one of those funny looking rifles over her shoulders and carrying homemade target boards in her hand. She moves like a gazelle towards the Land Rover.

She stashes her rifle in the back seat with me and slides into the front seat next to the driver and his rifle. Her rifle barrel is hot. She smiles a full smile as my fingers recoil from the gun's surface and then go back to cop a second feel. Breezy, bouncy Kurdish volleys back and forth as the driver turns the car around and heads back to Aunt Maya's. It is the first time I have heard the driver's voice. It is smothered, like he doesn't want anyone to hear him. Trahzia's swings as she speaks. All of her radiates vitality. She must have an entire other life outside Aunt Maya's kitchen.

As soon as we get home I head straight to my room, take off all my clothes, and stand in front of the full-length mirror in my cotton underwear. There is nothing gazelle like about me. Soft love handles droop over the elastic waist band of my bikini briefs. There is no space between my thighs when I stand with my feet together. Mom was pretty tall and Levi's thin. Then I sit down at my desk in front of a magnifying mirror. Annie is perched on the shelf above me. She watches as I study my face looking for traces of Mom. At certain angles I catch fleeting glimpses of her, and then she is gone, and I am left with my crowded reflection. My features seem too large for just one face. Annie slides herself onto my hand, hogs the mirror, and proclaims herself GOR-geous. Then she looks me up and down like a high school homecoming queen and returns to her shelf, shaking her beak from side to side.

Despite the heat, I change into sweat pants and a long-sleeved T-shirt, slip out the back door, cut across the marble-y stone patio, squeeze through some manicured bushes and exit the sub-division. It is the first time I have gone anywhere in Kurdistan by myself. Looking down at my covered arms and legs I realize just how much my life has changed since Mom died. My insides start to twist, so I pump my arms and legs to counteract the gut-spiraling. By the time I reach the highway I am drenched with sweat and choking on the smoky, dusty air. I chug across to the other side where a radio tower looms over dirty hills from its solitary perch. Hot, fat, saliva-y tears streak my chin as I push myself towards it. The Pit of Loneliness jacks to life as I hit the steep incline. Roaring, it opens its maniacal mouth as I gulp down air and propel myself up the hill.

At the top, the guard station in front of the tower is vacant. Beyond it, the land crests, then gives way to mustardy green fields lazing in the distance. A few straggler sheep graze downhill. I wonder where their flock mates have gone. My run putters to a walk as the tears subside and my left hand uncups a mouth that I don't remember covering. The Pit grates to a halt as my breathing slows and deepens. Suddenly, the sheep lift their heads as if responding to some unheard signal and obediently trot over the next ridge. I follow, scurrying through overgrown brittle brush that smells like sewer water.

Clearing the top of the next hill, I glimpse the trailing hem of a white robe rounding a bend. Tips of long, white hair float behind it. I sprint towards the apparition encouraged by a chorus of contented bleating. Around the other side, the yellow green field has molted, pearl gray puffs. Hundreds of sheep feed off the hillside. A young shepherd boy leaning on a wooden stick stares at me. I am suddenly grateful for sweatpants and long sleeves. A sugary breeze kicks up tickling under my chin. High atop a craggy cliff, the sun glints off something white, waving.

Every day I run over hills kicking up chalky dirt and avoiding camel spiders. Pushups and sit ups follow. When I feel like quitting, I picture the confidence in Trahzia's jaunty stride when she carries her rifle. I think about Mom having to hide in mountain caves and later sneak out of Kurdistan on foot. In the shadow of early evening with bats circling the street lights above, I outrun thoughts about what happened to her in between.

Aunt Maya's *Anfal* door panel series is being exhibited in Sami Abdulrahman Park. The exhibition is part of a "Reconciliation and Remembrance" conference featuring symposiums with international artists and humanitarian aid workers, and a field trip to Sulaimaniyah to the Red Security Museum. Aunt Maya is one of the guest speakers, so Trahzia and I get to go. The conference is held in the ballroom of the slick, shiny-polished Rotana Hotel and everyone who attends seems super-important. Trahzia and I sit next to each other on hard red velvet cushioned seats wearing oversized headphones attached to radio packs like the ones you get on museum tours. We tune into different channels for our respective languages, and when I get bored, I surf between Kurdish, Arabic, and English to see what I understand. There are mostly women in attendance, and the heady mix of perfume combined with the ripe smell of cigarette smoke from the corridor reminds me of going to one of Lila's gigs with Mom. Those days seem like a lifetime ago.

Aunt Maya takes the stage at 10:14 in a Calvin Klein suit and a hijab. It's like watching a badly dubbed movie because I see her speak but hear a male voice translating in my headset. Of course, she speaks in Kurdish; I don't know why I was expecting English. I am dumbfounded when she talks about the importance of honor, tradition, and forgiveness in maintaining the fabric of Kurdish society. My mind flashes to the mountain refugee camp photographs in Trahzia's album. I don't even realize I am shaking my head from side to side until Trahzia pats my hand. Her cool palms are smooth like rice paper. They don't match the bright coral of her nails. This is the first time I have seen her wear nail polish.

I wonder what Trahzia is thinking as we pile into a chartered bus and head for Sulaimaniyah. She fought for the Barzani tribe during *Anfal* and against them during the Kurdish civil war. Does this give her a wiser perspective? She wears the same placid look that she has when she is chopping vegetables. I sit in the back so I can watch other people decide where and whom to sit with. Sometimes life seems like an extension of high school. Aunt Maya and the conference organizer sit together up front. We exchange smiles across a sea of covered and uncovered heads. The air smells vaguely of feet.

The bus snakes southeast through pinky-red gorges dotted with small green bushes. Sometimes the hillside is lush, and the bus has to wait for a herd of sheep to cross the road. Other times it is scraggy and barren like the wind has lashed it for the last ten thousand years. We stop at the Geli Ali Beg Waterfall to take pictures and cool our feet. Then we continue on a road that dips and rises like a roller coaster so that my stomach meets my toes. Somewhere along the way I fall asleep and dream that I am the burnt little girl from Aunt Maya's door series but dressed in Scout's Halloween ham costume in *To Kill a Mockingbird*, and I'm trying to find my way home. The hills sprout trees as tall as radio towers strung with shiny silver prayer beads. All of the sudden a tree curtseys like a ballerina so I can climb on, then fully extends and passes me to a neighboring treetop. I treetop hop over meadows and deserts until I find a waterfall cascading into diamante crystals. I slide down into a cool pool that tastes like lemon ice.

The bus hits a sharp bump and jolts me awake. The inside of my mouth feels like hot cotton. Drool crusts the left side of my chin. Murmuring *bibure*, I lift my head from Trahzia's shoulder where it has imposed itself during my nap. She smiles at my awkward Kurdish word for sorry and hands me her bottle of water. The bus passes the manicured lawn of the American University of Sulaimaniyah, Iraq before it arrives at the bullet pock marked buildings surrounding the Red Security Museum, which is housed in one of Saddam's old torture facilities. There are dirt splattered tanks exhibited in the otherwise spartan courtyard. We enter through the Hall of Mirrors, which is decorated with 182,000 glass shards: one for each victim of *Anfal*, and 5,000 lights: one for each village wiped out by Saddam.

Inside the museum is a cold silence. There is almost no light. The air is thick and has no smell. There are torture rooms where men were stripped, hung up, and whipped into confessing. Remembering the long bumpy scars on the driver's back and shoulders, I look to see what Trahzia is doing, but she is not in this part of the exhibit. Next, we enter the raping room, where female suspects or the wives of male suspects at large were tortured. It is actually two small rooms. One is a kind of holding area where women were left to wait, and the other is a smaller room where the attacks were committed. That way the women in the holding area could listen to what was in store for them. Being in the raping room makes me feel like someone has stuffed me inside a burlap sack and pulled the drawstrings shut. I cross into the teen part of the prison and find a boy's crooked handwriting scrawled on a wall next to a bloody handprint. He is to be executed and claims that Saddam's men have forged his age so they can legally kill him. From the grave, he calls for someone to bear witness.

When I was nine, I got a wart on the middle section of my ring finger. When it became the size of an aspirin, I showed it to Mom. She took me down to the emergency room to have it burned out before it spread. The doctor tried to give me a shot of Novocain to numb my finger, but the needle was so big that I said no. Mom warned me that the burning was going to hurt worse than the shot, and that I should get it. Still I wouldn't give in. Mom tried to hold my other hand, but I wouldn't let her. I didn't close my eyes or look the other way. I watched as the wart was smoked off, charring my flesh, and my finger bled. Being in the Red Security Museum feels sort of like that.

I find Trahzia sitting on top of one of the tanks with a security guard. She is showing him his rifle. I smile at this and the burlap sack opens the teensiest bit. Even without a common language, I still know a lot about Trahzia. I know that she likes her weapons, both kitchen knives or rifles. I know she is as loyal to Aunt Maya as she is to the driver, and I am pretty sure those two were on opposite sides during the Kurdish civil war. Trahzia seems to have found reconciliation with the violence that scorched these brown hills and robbed them of their trees.

They say you never really know someone until you walk around in their shoes. Standing in the brown courtyard watching Aunt Maya pose with the guard and Trahzia, still holding his rifle, in front of the tank for a photo is a start.

~2~

The tenth-grade girls are drafted to perform a *chopy* dance at my school's open house. I beg Aunt Maya to get me out of it, but she says no. I can't tell if it's because she's a stickler for rules or she's hoping this will be the start of my embracing Kurdish culture. In any case, as much as I practice with Trahzia, I just can't get it right. At rehearsal I hang out with Zerin and Glara, two other Kurdish-American girls. Zerin is from San Diego, and Glara is from Texas. They both have moms. They can wear makeup and put their own pictures on their Facebook pages. They can't do the *chopy*. Whenever we crash into each other at practice, we have to say one thing we miss about back home.

On Saturday morning at 9:59, the driver takes Aunt Maya, Trahzia, and me to the citadel. I need a traditional costume to perform the *chopy* in, and Aunt Maya can't be more excited. I am excited to see the citadel. People have lived there for over 6,000 years, which includes the Assyrian period of rule in Kurdistan. Maybe I'll find a book about Mar Yosip.

At the citadel, I see very few foreigners. After we clamber up ancient broken steps and duck under stone arches, we head to the central square which surrounds a massive water fountain. In its cooling mists, women in *abayas* pose for pictures with their children. Some men are enjoying bulb-shaped glasses of sugary black tea while smoking *shisha* pipes, which gurgle with every inhale. Try as I might, I can't imagine Mom in this place.

Next, we head to the fabric part of the bazaar. There is a constant smell of BO. The walkways are narrow and throng with people. Some of them stare. Others whip out cell phones and take our picture. Some people recognize Aunt Maya and pressure us into their shops. I am amazed at how polite and smiley she is with all of them. Mom never had that kind of patience, especially in crowded malls. She would have been muttering under her breath.

Aunt Maya finally chooses a fabric shop. Inside there are too many options. Bolts upon bolts of brightly colored fabric vie for attention. I deliberately stare to blur my vision and let instinct guide me through the fuzzy choices towards a bolt of water-colored fabric with rhinestones. It is not until Aunt Maya hands the tailor a cloth-framed photograph of two young red-haired girls that I understand why I chose it. He points to Mom in the photo, then at me, and says *dayik*. My smile back to him is wavy. She was my mother; is she still? I agree to the same long dress thingy over floaty pants, but draw a line at the hijab. Aunt Maya seems content with this. She one-arm hugs me around the shoulders. I let her and forget to look for a book on Mar Yosip.

The next week Trahzia and the driver take me to pick up my costume. We stop at a *shawarma* shop for something to eat. The place is teeming with families. Little children try not to spill on their shirt fronts while people pass napkins, hot sauce, and yoghurt cucumber topping from table to table. The smell of spices, grilled *kifta*, deep fried falafel, and too many bodies mingle together. The table tops are sticky. On the pickup counter lay a few stray fries. This is somewhere I can picture Mom eating but not Aunt Maya. I wonder if Trahzia was their glue. Someday I am going to learn enough Kurdish to ask her.

We arrive at the tailor's at 11:37. I change into my sea-swirl-blue costume. The running and the pushups and the sit-ups have had an effect. I look more like Mom and yet not. Trahzia loops her arm through mine and drags me to *chopy* in front of a full-length mirror. For a moment I can't tell if she is in the past or the present. The tailor watches for a while and says something in syncopated Kurdish. Trahzia meets his gaze in the mirror, nodding yes. The tailor comes closer and joins our *chopy* line. Looping his arm through mine, he says, You must to put your shoulders all in, and then he demonstrates.

I try it. He is right. You must put all in.

Mosul

AFTER THE BABY DIED, SANNA BEGAN CLEANING. She washed the dishes, and the linens, and at night, the windows at the shelter. She scrubbed the floors. She keeps her hands busy.

She beats a worn cloth against the corridor floor. Sometimes this floor is speckled with dirt, sometimes with shit, sometimes with blood. She washes these floors twice a day. No one tells her to.

"A woman wants to see you," a security guard says. Sanna wrings the soapy water from the rag, lets the suds dribble over her knuckles and wrists.

"Why?" Few people visit the shelter.

Heels click onto the tiles and into Sanna's field of vision. Sanna's eyes travel the length of the woman's slim cut trousers to her short hair unabashedly uncovered. The woman haunches down and introduces herself in Arabic. She sways slightly and Sanna resists her urge to steady this stranger.

The woman holds out her hand to Sanna's soiled one. "My name is Rashida. I am organizing a gallery show of art work by women in shelters. I understand you are quite clever with your hands,"—now Sanna's eyes flick directly at the woman's—"I want you to make something for our show." The woman's self-confidence expands her smile. Sanna ignores her outstretched palm and washes the floor.

The request is incredible. Most locals view the shelter as *haram* and would prefer its inhabitants to be below rather than above ground. Sanna smiles. What kind of art work could she create from the plastic forks and knives she washes nightly? She scrubs a permanent spot on the tile.

"The show is part of a conference, to raise awareness about violence against women." The explanation is greeted by the dunking and dribbling of Sanna's rag.

Rashida tentatively wraps her hand around Sanna's and they wash the floor together. The saturated rag makes patterns on the tiles. "It's like painting. Covering and uncovering, exposing the underneath." They work silently together and Rashida does not seem to notice the water and dirt staining the knees of her trousers. "I have done this type of show before. Would you like to see some pictures?"

Sanna thinks the artwork is humiliating: there are collages made from marker colored plastic forks, crudely beaded jewelry, glittered Styrofoam sculptures. Abruptly backing away, she overturns the bucket. Suds streak across the floor. Sanna envies their movement.

"I am also a lawyer," Rashida says, switching to Kurdish. "I could counsel women here while I work on the show."

Sanna silently counts the number of beds at the shelter. Some are double occupied. There is one part-time legal advisor and too little bribe money to help all these young women. She feels the phantom sensation of Rashida's hand holding her own. "Can you get me clay?" Sanna relished the power she feels when she molds the milky-muddy substance.

Ten months earlier in Erbil, Banu had entered Sanna's bedroom window, bloodied and crying. As best friends, it was not unusual for the two to share a bed, a flashlight between them, but usually at Banu's house. Sanna's brother Mohammad had a temper that flattened his eyes and disappeared his lips. When left alone with him, Sanna usually kept a chair wedged against her bedroom door handle.

Wordlessly, Sanna cleaned Banu's split lip, her crusted and swollen eye, the dried blood between her legs. With Banu's honor stolen, she couldn't return to her family. The girls mimed sleep until daybreak. Neither knew where she was going.

During her next visit, Rashida produces the clay, along with a laptop, scanner and printer. Sanna marvels at the technology. She wants to surf the internet. More primal is her need to squeeze the clay, to form something out of nothing. Instead, she takes Rashida on a tour of the shelter.

The dormitory is eerily quiet; its air is feral. The girls assume their bodies are shadows as their eyes track Rashida's movements through the room. Sanna watches Rashida make her rounds.

"Are these all of the girls residing at the shelter?" Rashida asks. About three quarters of the beds seat spectators, the rest are unmade or claimed by meager belongings strewn across blankets. One remains untouched.

"Some of the girls are watching TV; some are in the reading room. We try not to move around too much during the day. Not all of the windows are heavily curtained."

"It's like a sanctuary."

Sanna really looks at Rashida. With her defiantly cropped hair and fitted trousers, Sanna didn't think Rashida was religious. Now she wonders why Rashida has come here at all.

Five years earlier, in the evening of December 13, 2003, the evening Operation Red Dawn captured Saddam Hussein in a spider hole near Tikrit, Sanna returned home to her family's modest apartment in Stockholm with an invitation to the Royal Institute of Art's Gifted Program folded inside her left mitten and a bag of Swedish gummy fish hidden in her right. Snow powdered the air as she gnawed a rubbery tail debating which parent to beg first. Opening the apartment door, Sanna was bowled over by the fragrance of *biryani* and *dolma*, food her mother usually prepared for traditional celebrations. Sanna's mother stood while her brother sat transfixed by the TV, which was usually silent during dinnertime. It had been moved from the living room to the kitchen table. Sanna could hear her father speaking Kurdish on the telephone in his office down the hall. An unkempt and disheveled Saddam emerging from the dirty earth played in an endless loop scored by newscaster commentary. Sanna caressed the edges of the invitation before she withdrew her hands from her mittens and left her future possibilities behind in the foyer. With Saddam no longer killing Kurds, the family would be returning to northern Iraq.

Rashida nods at the security guard as she exits the shelter. Her driver Hamzeh makes no move to put out his cigarette as she approaches the car. She opens the door and sits in the backseat with the butt of Hamzeh's Kalashnikov rifle against her calf. She will not let the driver's disapproval of her work at the shelter irritate her because he knows *Pesh Merga* guards at every checkpoint from Mosul to Erbil. None of them suspect Hamzeh used to provide security for Saddam's personal pilots, which included her father.

Rashida consults her notes as Hamzeh drives. There should have been 23 girls at the shelter, but Rashida had counted only 22 during her tour. Rashida already knows that the missing girl is Banu, that Sanna knows Banu has gone and sidestepped the question, and that no one sleeps in that meticulously made bed. Now she wants to know why. Banu's parents want to know too. They've invested a lot of money into Rashida's gallery show to find out.

After Rashida leaves, Sanna takes the clay into the bathroom, locks the door, and works at softening it. She hasn't molded in ages and her fingers ache from the exertion. She thinks about the last time they throbbed this much, when Banu held them so tightly Sanna thought they would break. With her left hand wrapped around one of the metal bars and her right hand wrapped around Sanna's fingers, it was the night Banu gave birth to a little boy with Sanna subbing as a midwife. Two other inmates supported Banu's weight while a third massaged her swollen belly. The baby slid onto the cell's mud floor amidst fluid and blood; urine and shit. After that, Banu slept.

Sanna held the baby to Banu's breast to nurse him as she lay unconscious. There was something familiar in the slope of his nose that lightened Sanna. She held the baby close and described Stockholm, described the snow that purified the city overnight when no one was looking.

When Banu finally awoke, she stared at Sanna and the baby with contempt. How could she play with it? Sanna may not have realized that it was Mohammed who had raped Banu that night Banu crawled through Sanna's window, but looking at the baby now, how could Sanna help but see it? The baby had the slant of his father's eyes, the prominent shape of his nose, the determined set of his chin. Mohammed had been watching Banu for years, waiting. No one had wanted Banu to marry Sanna's brother, but the attack changed that. Culture and tradition demanded Banu marry Mohammed to resolve a blood feud between families and restore her honor. Being pregnant and deciding to run away instead put Banu behind bars. Sanna's complicity made her collateral damage.

"Don't you want to hold him?" Sanna offered.

"I want it dead," Banu whispered turning toward the wall.

"Banu," Sanna started.

"What?" The force of her voice caused it to reverberate inside their cell. "It should have never lived. I should have never lived. Your brother should have killed me when he stole my virtue."

Sanna stared down at the baby nestled on her chest and saw traces of Mohammed twinning within its face. Swallowing Banu's name, Sanna thrust the baby away from her. "Please!" She held out the baby towards its mother. Banu shoved him back towards Sanna. As the baby fumbled out of Sanna's arms, Sanna grabbed his head around its neck before the baby hit the ground. Banu fastened her hands over Sanna's and pressed them together. Sanna looked in Banu's eyes and saw nothing. She tried to shake Banu off, but Banu pressed harder. Hand over hand, the two girls squeezed the breath out of the baby. His lips turned blue; his eyes never opened. When he stilled, Banu took him from Sanna, put him on her sleeping mat, lay down next to him, and closed her eyes. Sanna crumpled where she stood and curled into herself. She was jarred into wakefulness by Banu's screaming. Banu did not stop wailing until she and Sanna were taken to a nearby mosque for consolation. The girls ran during the evening call to prayer.

True to her word, Rashida visits the shelter almost daily to provide legal counsel and supervise artwork. Sanna doesn't question how she smuggles in carving tools or procures Western art supplies. She is determined to enjoy her luxuries while they last. She knows that Rashida and whatever organization that funds her will eventually lose interest.

Rashida watches Sanna sketch what her installation will look like. It's up to Rashida to make sure it happens. Sanna has requested a half meter by two-meter black box be built to house her creative entry. She has already molded life size scales of justice out of clay. Upon entering the black box, a viewer steps onto one of the scale's dishes. His weight tips the scale, which Sanna has rigged to pivot. Inside the black box hang dozens of glow-in-the-dark plastic knives adorned with the names of women who are incarcerated because they refused their attackers. On the floor of the black box are tiny clay babies that are randomly crushed by the scale.

"It's visceral and gutsy Sanna. I understand why the Royal Institute of Art wanted you. Maybe you'll get there yet."

By now Sanna has learned not to be surprised by all that Rashida knows. "Maybe," Sanna works in silence. "Or maybe I'll reach an honorable conclusion when I step outside this shelter." Sanna stops sketching and starts packing up the art supplies.

"Sanna, I understand how you feel." Although Rashida's voice is controlled, her left jaw tendon quivers. Sanna becomes aware of the kitchen clock ticking. Then a manicured hand hesitates on her forearm. "Tell me what happened to Banu." Rashida's voice is not quite a plea.

The baby's death pushed Banu down the rabbit hole. After they ran, Banu stole food to keep her and Sanna alive. She dishonored herself to keep them alive. She pulled Sanna along, all the while thanking Sanna for killing it, for freeing them. Her sing-song babble muted Sanna. Eventually they found their way to the shelter in Mosul.

After, at the shelter, Banu tore at her hair. She laughed at nothing until she choked. She hid things, broke things, bullied. She stopped showering, stopped eating, stopped speaking. Then Banu was gone.

"I don't know." As Sanna shuffles out of Rashida's reach, Rashida almost believes her.

Long after the gallery show has ended, Sanna will wait at the shelter for Banu's return.

Ras al-Amud

ONE FRIDAY EVENING, nineteen-year-old Yasmeen Al-Hashimy counts to 378 before a wave of contractions sends her squatting next to a green sofa back, hugging its worn edges for support. Time hovers. Her belly is gluey with sweat under her T-shirt and *thobe*. Somewhere a neighbor is frying falafel. The smell of coriander and turmeric snakes through the living room causing Yasmeen's saliva to sour. Through the living room window, she sees the Holy City's fortress walls cut like jagged teeth against the sky. Behind them, the Dome of the Rock glows phosphorus. She considers waiting for her husband Ahmad to return from the mosque before leaving for the hospital, but the next contraction crescendos, pulling Yasmeen to the tile in its undertow.

One *salamu alakuum*, two *salamu alakuum*, three *salamu alakuum*. She counts underneath the muezzin's *adhan*. She phones Ahmad. He must have silenced his mobile for the sunset call to prayer. She sends a text, grabs her identity card and pocketbook, and hauls her hopper-ball belly down the stairs to the roundabout by the Ras al-Amud Mosque hoping to glimpse Ahmad before hailing a shared taxi. The few cabs that are on the road are packed tight.

Yasmeen doubles over with the next contraction. A silver door handle glides into view. It is attached to a shiny black car that has stopped alongside her. A window rolls down. Over French pop music she hears an Islamic greeting and an invitation to get in. Levelling herself with the window, Yasmeen tastes the cool air inside the car. A single bead of sweat escapes from under her hijab. Her hands whisper over her head to make sure her headscarf is secure while the driver's gleaming fingernails alight on the steering wheel. Dismissing a pack of Gitanes cigarettes on the dashboard, Yasmeen lowers herself into the back seat and exhales the name of her hospital. The car smells of coconut and imitation Armani. She concentrates on breathing.

Beyond the roundabout, the sunbaked asphalt clogs with cars approaching the separation wall. Open-bed trucks carrying Palestinian grapes, figs, and prickly pears from the Jordan Valley are stalled on the other side of the checkpoint where their fruit will spoil in the open heat in a few days' time. A ribbon of cars extends from both sides of the crossing towards the horizon.

Yasmeen's pelvis feels like it is separating. The pain flashes white and squeezes her. The back seat seems to twirl from left to right. What might be two minutes passes until the next contraction. Moments vanish during a breath. She pants in time to Nouvelle Vague's "In a Manner of Speaking" coming from the stereo.

"Lie back," the driver suggests as he hands her an opened bottle of water. Hair gel separates his black curls. Yasmeen presses the bottle to her forehead. Cars slow to a crawl. Few horns dare protest this close to the Israel Defense Forces manning the checkpoint.

Yasmeen cries out with the next set of contractions. The car rolls two meters forward and stops. It vibrates beneath them. There are twenty-two cars between her and any one of the four Israeli soldiers who should wave the car through to the access road that winds twenty-six kilometers around settlements and their security buffer zones to her hospital, which is twelve kilometers from her apartment. By the time the driver's car reaches the IDF guards, her contractions are ninety-two seconds apart, and she longs for a toilet.

"Give me your identity cards within five seconds," orders a soldier accompanied by a thirsty-looking German shepherd. Her voice shakes her words. When Yasmeen and the driver take more than five seconds, the soldier hands their cards back to them.

"Do it again. Five seconds. Mark. Go." She takes a giant step backwards from the car. Her eyes flick to her right where the checkpoint commander, a man who looks capable of great violence, is smoking. The cherry on the commander's cigarette burns a brighter red with his inhalation.

"One, two, three, four, five." An open hand extends just beyond the driver's reach. The soldier steps forward to snatch the cards from the driver's fingers, and then drops them through his open window when she hands them back. They land somewhere under the brake pedal. The driver's left jaw tendon spasms as his fingers stumble blindly along the carpet. His nostrils flare.

"Last chance." She starts counting before the driver has picked them up. "Onetwothreefourfive." The numbers run together like a pack of stray dogs. "Sixseveneightnineteneleventwelve." When he finally hands them to her, she disappears with Yasmeen's and the driver's cards for three sets of contractions eighty-seven, eight-three, and seventy-nine seconds apart.

When the soldier returns, she hands them back their cards. "Don't you see you're delaying the people behind you? You need to learn not to waste other people's time. End of the line."

Before the driver can turn the car around, Yasmeen lets loose an animal sound and the smell of mulched vegetables fills the car's interior. Yasmeen's face rusts. The driver swings the car door open and places one foot on the graveled pavement. Throwing his cigarette to the ground, the commander points his M16 in the driver's direction and covers the space with two long strides. The barrel of his rifle comes level with the driver's nostrils. Time stretches.

"Why did you advance on my soldier?" He pushes the rifle a few inches closer to the driver's face. "I could pull this trigger." The driver has become a statue. His eyes resist the draw of the gun's barrel. "Hands on top of your head." Another gun covers Yasmeen and the driver as the commander pulls the driver from the car. He sees Yasmeen's watermelon belly. "Fuck! Get her out of the car. Have the dog search it." The commander cuffs the driver with zip ties and leaves him standing in the sun. The light is low, orange, and merciless. The commander turns off the ignition and stashes the keys on the car's roof.

Yasmeen's heart opens and closes very quickly inside her chest as the soldier grabs her under her arms and yanks her out of the backseat. Her *thobe* is stained wet where she was sitting. Her water has broken and she smells feral. The German shepherd heads for Yasmeen's crotch. Yasmeen's blood swarms for a panicked moment until the soldier redirects the dog towards the car. Shadows lengthen as the sun skims the separation wall.

The dog finds nothing. Time skids. Approaching cars extend the standstill line. The checkpoint is a wilderness of vehicles. An ambulance is called. The commander cuts the zip ties, returns the car keys, and sends the car and its passengers to a waiting area off at the side. The driver turns his steering wheel as birds cross the sky like souls.

As he increases the distance between himself and the commander, fear creeps back down the driver's throat. A single blue vein throbs lengthwise bisecting his forehead. He needs to smoke. God is great. The pregnant woman's pungent water masked the Vaseline-encased marijuana bags hidden inside the backseat cushions.

He checks her progress in the rearview mirror. Where is her husband? He remembers how her hands settled her hijab before she climbed into the backseat, how her eyes darted to his cigarettes and faltered, how long she waited to lie back. She is not a dishonorable woman. What has she seen of life? Her eyes look young and old at the same time. What is her name? He knows better than to ask. In his line of work, exchanging names can break a person. "I don't think your baby will wait for the ambulance." His voice is like warm oil. "I can take you to a friend. He's a doctor on this side of the checkpoint."

Yasmeen's legs fight her modesty and spread. She croaks out a yes and reaches for her mobile to call Ahmad now that the sky is the color of the sea. She concentrates on the pinpoints of oncoming headlights travelling between dirt splotches on the windshield.

Time ripples. Pain is a red-yellow flame licking at the edges of everything. The car stops. Someone drips cold water into her mouth and across her forehead. Ahmad's voice is in her ear. The smell of their fabric softener. Two sets of hands lift her from the car and carry her. The clap of hard-soled shoes on stone streets. Metal grates rattling shut. A child's shriek. Sounds braid.

Up steps, around a corner, then straight. A hard turn. More steps. Cooler air blankets her. A sharp knock. Only once. A door opens. Shadows giving way to light. The harsh smell of antiseptic. New voices, hushed. A small prick in her arm. Someone takes her hand and brings it to his lips. Her fingers graze a five o'clock shadow: Ahmad. She freefalls into softness.

Beneath her are floating cushions. Voices come to her from the end of a long tunnel. She wraps her lips around the sounds she hears to decipher their secret code. Rummaging in her mind for a word, she understands that several voices are telling her to push. She feels the skin of not quite her upper thigh and not quite her pelvis flutter like a moth as it tears millimeter by millimeter. Pain glows outward in pulsating circles. Her insides are slippery fire. Her eyes focus on long square fingers that disappear between her legs. She feels them turn something inside her. The fingers belong to the hands of a man she has never seen before. A flash of panic. He pulls as he tells her to push. A shadow of a memory flits past her: there, then not. To her left she sees Ahmad's eyebrows knit into a caterpillar. His dark saucer eyes hold frozen tears. His lips round. *Push.* Muscles stretching. Ripping. *Push.* She pushes until what was inside her is outside her, and the Yasmeen that is left is no bigger than a girl.

The baby, a boy, has blue skin. He wears an umbilical cord necklace. The room hushes. He does not move. He does not cry. He does not make friends with life. Yasmeen's heart is suffocating. She turns her face away from her husband's tender head collapsed upon her bosom. His tears soak into her T-shirt, wetting the skin covering her breastbone. She does not stroke his head. She does not soothe him. Her insides have been raked. A metallic bitter taste gloves her tongue.

ᒪ

The earth rotates a tiny bit further. Back at their apartment, rooms shrink. Passing between the green sofa and TV, Yasmeen steps on Ahmad's foot. While he puts groceries away, Ahmad's elbow knocks Yasmeen's rib cage. Their mattress widens from the middle, leaving them on opposite edges of a tiny world. Words disintegrate across their bed and become the hum under a seashell.

The bedroom clock ticks. Ahmad reaches across the expanse of mattress for Yasmeen as she cocoons inward. There is a damp look on her face, grief or hate, it's hard to say. He wants to hold her close, smell the amber and honey of her soap on his skin. Something in his chest tightens.

Time slows; the walls fade away. She is lying above him, her soft charcoal eyes dancing, her waterfall of hair shielding them from everything. She traces his mouth with her thumb, sliding its padded tip over his lips to his whiskered chin. Her warm breath sprinkles baby names into his ear. He lingers in memory until his heart unfists itself.

The walls return; they feel tenuous. Under night's stillness, he listens to Yasmeen's measured breath in sleep, watches her face, motionless except for its eyelids. Stroking a lock of her hair between his thumb and forefinger, Ahmad wills his wife to come back to herself. The woman beside him radiating intense heat as she slumbers is both Yasmeen and not.

More revolutions around the clock. Silence sets itself at the dinner table. Ahmad returns to his professorship, studying the past to understand the present. Yasmeen wants to erase the past, obliterate spirals of memory until there is nothing left but this moment beaded to the next. No shared history. No heart-breaking complexity. The loss of the son has drained all feeling for the father. Yasmeen is an empty Russian nesting doll, brittle and hollow. When Ahmad suggests they try again, she fills with bile.

Time zigzags. Two blue blankets with friendly yellow ducks, fourteen cloud-soft onesies, a garden of flower-embroidered hats, a tiny mountain of hand-knit booties. One large cocoa-colored bear as big as Yasmeen's sternum snuggles in her lap. Perched on the nursery floor, Yasmeen folds impossibly small T-shirts. She takes down the musical mobile of prismatic stars. She gathers bibs and burp cloths and hooded towels, and packs everything into a tidy garbage bag. The bear is the last to go. She lies back among the wasteland of her failed pregnancy and balances the bear on the soles of her feet. Her legs extend and stretch. One, two, three, the bear is flying. On the underside of her eyelids a soundless movie plays: a boy crawling across tile to the green sofa, using it to pull himself up. That slow, wobbly first step forward. His candied breath warming her cheek with kisses. Tiny, trusting fingers wrapped around her wrist as they walk to his first day of school. Yasmeen's heart swells, pushing up into her throat. She cannot swallow. The film cuts. Her eyes open. The midday call to prayer wisps into the room as Yasmeen finishes packing.

The old city is a maze of noise and fragrance. Two IDF guards—one tall, one not—wearing ceramic bullet proof vests stand just inside the Damascus Gate, patrolling the main entrance to the Muslim Quarter. Raw sunlight beats down on Yasmeen's head as she twines through slivered streets, heading for a charity shop. When she nears the Damascus Gate, her eyes lock on the soldiers' faces bronzed from the sun. Why are they laughing? The tall one's tiny square teeth do not match the architecture of his head. The small one spits over his right shoulder and laughs again. What right do they have to laugh? Yasmeen hugs the bag full of baby things to her chest while her thoughts flutter like caged butterflies. Tears heat the back of her throat. Her heartbeat thuds in her ears. In wondrous slowness, another version of herself rushes the guards and dumps the contents of the bag in front of their feet. *Look at what you did.* The teddy bear falls out first and lands backside up pointed towards the Western Wall. The butt of an M16 connects with Yasmeen's head. Everything dims.

Pictures flit back and forth and spin: the bear's decapitated head leaking stuffing, the musical mobile smashed into kaleidoscope glory, baby booties soaking up puddles of reddish- brown water in front of a *shawarma* shop. When she lifts her head from the pavement, Yasmeen's skull pounds. Her shoulders tear at the sockets; her hands are zip-tied behind her back. Dust-filmed combat boots inch towards her belly. Her thoughts untangle. She is close enough to spit on those shoes if she dares.

"What were you thinking?" The tall soldier laces his fingers across his utility belt. His giant frame blocks the sun. "You could have been shot. We didn't know what you had in that bag."

Tick. Tick. Tick. Tick. Tick. Yasmeen says nothing. The not tall soldier watches from a distance. Yasmeen focuses on the bear's button eye and waits as patient as a stone. She feels the sun warm her face when the soldier squats down. Snip. Snip. Blood flows into her wrists and hands.

"Are you OK?"

Yasmeen's heart beats in confusion. A hard-faced woman in a faded *thobe* picks up the duck blankets and stuffs them into a plastic bag. Somewhere a boy's throaty, high-pitched voice announces fig juice for sale. Yasmeen's gaze slides to the tall soldier. His face flows with concern. Doubt slips around her like eels.

"Can you stand?"

Yasmeen doesn't expect the soldier to extend his hand, nor does she expect to take it. Who knows which surprises her more? Something inside her loosens. Blood gallops to her head as she stands under the bowl of the sky. Its edges go dark and fuzzy. Her ankles are wobbly. She grasps his hand a moment longer. His palms are dry and smooth in the afternoon heat. He steadies her. "*Shukran*," she whispers before snatching her hand back.

The soldier smiles his tiny-toothed smile. "*Afwan*." And just like that, he lets Yasmeen go.

She wanders the labyrinth of shops as daylight unravels. Polygons of wild blue sky flow behind corrugated tin awnings. Yasmeen's eyes graze on mermaid-colored Roman glass snow-flaked with patina. The song of hawkers resounds down the lanes and resonates through her belly. Something too-long dormant and exquisitely fragile bubbles under her skin.

She sweeps from counter to counter as she samples dried apricots, fresh almonds, and agrarian basil. Anything with color. Anything with fragrance. Sweet cheese pastries taste like clouds; honey is a drizzle of thick sunlight rained to earth. Next to Yasmeen, a Western woman in a sleeveless sundress, maybe American, orders baklava in accented Arabic. Her toned arms are golden; her uncovered head is sun-streaked. She wears no wedding band. On the black screen of her imagination, Yasmeen feels sunrays lap at her skin and warm her hair. She fills with a voluptuous panic. She envisions herself buying sweets in a foreign market, unencumbered, free.

The muezzin of the al-Aqsa mosque announces the sunset call to prayer, pulling Yasmeen from her reverie. To her right, a penguin of a woman in a black hijab negotiates a price for grape leaves. Yasmeen imagines the woman's claw-like fingers mixing minced lamb meat with lemon scented rice for *dolma* stuffing. She sees the woman smooth a delicate grape leaf on top of her kitchen counter, spoon on the rice and meat concoction, fold neat, square corners into the sides of the leaf and roll, repeating the sequence until the bottom of her pan is covered in tight, green cigars.

To Yasmeen's left a young mother, who could be Yasmeen's twin, wrestles with her two- year-old son to seat him in his stroller. The son bellows, exercising the full force of his tiny lungs. He does not want to sit! He wants to explore. Yasmeen eyes the mother's belly, round with her second. Yasmeen's face empties. Something in her heart clicks shut: a captured infinite. Moments slip away under the muezzin's *iqama*. As the devout line up for the beginning of prayer, Yasmeen drifts home. The sun edges from the day.

～

Ahmad waits in the dark kitchen's silence. From somewhere come the muted sounds of dinnertime: muffled voices, clanking silver, sporadic laughter. His own table is bare.

The front door sighs open and coughs. The jangle of keys. Light footsteps murmur over the tile. The kitchen light snaps on. Ahmad blinks likes a caged animal in the harshness of its glare.

"Where were you?" His voice reverberates in the hushed room.

"In the old city." The apartment reeks of sameness. Yasmeen starts washing green beans for *fasoulya khadra*. Water rumbles from the tap. A pot of water is set to boil.

"Yasmeen, what happened to all the baby things?" Ahmad's voice breaks.

Snap. Snap. Snap. Snap. Yasmeen halves the beans.

Ahmad's hands are on her shoulders. He turns her towards him. Yasmeen's eyes affix to the wall behind his left ear, to his slippered feet, to anywhere but his gaze. Ahmad takes her chin and tilts her face to his. He does not remove his hand. She concentrates on the follicles of dark hair just breaking the skin's surface above his upper lip. His face is shiny with the day's heat.

"What happened to the baby things?"

"I gave them away." Yasmeen's voice is a susurration.

"What?"

"I gave them away in the old city." She does not mention the bump on the back of her head nor the soldier who helped her stand.

"You had no right to do that."

"I couldn't look at them anymore."

"Yasmeen. We'll have a child. We'll have plenty of them. We have our whole lives."

Yasmeen backs up from Ahmad's embrace. She keeps her eyes focused on the acreage of his chest. "I don't know."

"What do you mean? It's our dream. Little ones of our own."

"I don't know if it's my dream anymore." The ensuing silence coats them.

Ahmad clears his throat. "Since when?"

"Since that," Yasmeen's breath skips, "night." Something inside her pulls taut.

Ahmad moves forward. Again, his arms encircle her. Again, she backs away. They two- step from the sink to the refrigerator. The water boils, rattling its pot on the burner.

"*Habibti,* you're grieving. We both are. I lost him too." Ahmad's voice is a scratch beneath the floorboards. "But I love you and I know you love me, and someday you'll want to try again."

Yasmeen says nothing. She watches the scene as though observing actors in a stage play. The call to *Isha* prayer weaves through the kitchen. Ahmad's lips move in whispered recitation as he readies himself for the mosque. *There is no strength or power except from God.* Yasmeen wonders how much is faith, how much is habit, and how much is fear.

"I'm going to pray for guidance. You know your place is here with me." His eyes are a limpid eternity. "I love you, Yasmeen." The apartment door clicks shut.

Yasmeen resumes making dinner. She blanches the beans, turning them a lucent shade of green. The last bright thing inside her flickers. Outside her kitchen window, moonlight shatters against the Dome of the Rock. Inside her chest pulses something broken but unafraid.

Credits

The stories "V", "Kurdistan," and "Ras al-Amud" were originally published in the book, *Girl, World*, published by Laughing Fire Press. ISBN: 978-0996490559

The story "Jinwar" began as the short story, "Room 308," which was published by the *Laurel Review* and is included in the collection *Girl, World*, first published by Laughing Fire Press.

The story "V" was first published by *Short Fiction: The Visual Literary Journal* and included in the collection *Girl, World*, first published by Laughing Fire Press.

The story "Kurdistan" was first published by *Prick of the Spindle* and included in the collection *Girl, World*, first published by Laughing Fire Press.

The story "Mosul" was commended for the Baker Prize and included in its 2014 anthology of winners.

The story "Ras al-Amud" was first published by *Litro* and included in the collection *Girl, World*, first published by Laughing Fire Press.

These credits are a continuation of the "Credits" section of the Copyright Page. For more, go to the Copyright page.

Disclaimer

Acknowledgements

BOOKS DO NOT WRITE THEMSELVES. I am forever indebted to the people who inspire my stories and the places which spark my imagination.

I was compelled to write the title novella, *Jinwar* after hearing the stories of survivors of rape in the military. My hope is that people will read this story and pressure their congressmen to endorse a bill to take rape cases out of the military's chain of command and put them in a separate military tribunal, which already exists to adjudicate other types of cases.

I want to thank all my students, especially the young women I have had the privilege of teaching. You have taught me how to look at the world with wonder and awe.

Thanks to Tony, Karen, and Ellen for reading drafts and offering your invaluable feedback, which made my stories stronger. Thanks to Baron for his support and introductions.

Thanks to the Chicago writers' community, who have been very generous with their support of my work, and to Sheryl, who facilitated my meeting many of the fabulous writers working and living in the Windy City and for her exceptional generosity and unwavering support.

Thanks to the Writers Studio, New York, where I learned everything I know about writing.

Thanks to my mother and late father, to whom I owe everything.

About Cune Press

CUNE PRESS WAS FOUNDED IN 1994 to publish thoughtful writing of public importance. Our name is derived from "cuneiform." (In Latin *cuni* means "wedge.")

In the ancient Near East the development of cuneiform script—simpler and more adaptable than hieroglyphics—enabled a large class of merchants and landowners to become literate. Clay tablets inscribed with wedge-shaped stylus marks made possible a broad inter-meshing of individual efforts in trade and commerce.

Cuneiform enabled scholarship to exist and art to flower, and created what historians define as the world's first civilization. When the Phoenicians developed their sound-based alphabet, they expressed it in cuneiform.

The idea of Cune Press is the democratization of learning, the faith that rarefied ideas, pulled from dusty pedestals and displayed in the streets, can transform the lives of ordinary people. And it is the conviction that ordinary people, trusted with the most precious gifts of civilization, will give our culture elasticity and depth—a necessity if we are to survive in a time of rapid change.

Books from Cune Press

 Aswat: Voices from a Small Planet (a series from Cune Press)
Looking Both Ways   Pauline Kaldas
Stage Warriors   Sarah Imes Borden
Stories My Father Told Me   Helen Zughraib

 Syria Crossroads (a series from Cune Press)
Leaving Syria   Bill Dienst & Madi Williamson
Visit the Old City of Aleppo   Khaldoun Fansa
The Dusk Visitor   Musa Al-Halool
Steel & Silk   Sami Moubayed
Syria - A Decade of Lost Chances   Carsten Wieland
The Road from Damascus   Scott C. Davis
A Pen of Damascus Steel   Ali Ferzat
White Carnations   Musa Rahum Abbas

 Bridge Between the Cultures (a series from Cune Press)
Confessions of a Knight Errant   Gretchen McCullough
Afghanistan & Beyond   Linda Sartor
Apartheid is a Crime   Mats Svensson
The Passionate Spies   John Harte
Congo Prophet   Frederic Hunter
Music Has No Boundaries   Rafique Gangat

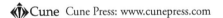 Cune Press: www.cunepress.com

ALEX POPPE IS THE AUTHOR of three other works of fiction: *Duende* (2022), *Moxie* (2019), and *Girl, World* (2017). *Girl, World* was named a 35 Over 35 Debut Book Award winner, First Horizon Award finalist, Montaigne Medal finalist, short-listed for the Eric Hoffer Grand Prize and was awarded an Honorable Mention in General Fiction from the Eric Hoffer Awards.

Her short fiction has been a finalist for *Glimmer Train's* Family Matters contest, a nominee for the Push-cart Prize and commended for the Baker Prize among others. Her non-fiction was named a Best of the Net nominee (2016), a finalist for *Hot Metal Bridge's* Social Justice Writing contest and has appeared in *The Los Angeles Review, The Laurel Review, Bust, Medium's The Startup,* and *Bella Caledonia* among others.

She is a staff writer at Preemptive Love and has completed her third and fourth books of fiction with support from Can Serrat International Art Residency and Duplo-Linea De Costa Artist in Residency programs. She was thrilled to be an artist-in-residence at the Atlantic Center for the Arts in spring 2021. When she is not being thrown from the back of food aid trucks or dining with pistol-packing Kurdish hit men, she writes.

For more: www.alexpoppe.com

Alex Poppe, trained as an actress, gave up her career and in a courageous move few Western women would dare to make, went alone to Iraq and became a teacher, fulfilled a dream and became a writer. Her story is inspiring and her talent is clear and her writing is bold and vivid.

—Jere Van Dyk,
The Trade: My Journey into the Labyrinth of Political Kidnapping;
The New York Times, National Geographic, CBS News

CPSIA information can be obtained
at www.ICGtesting.com
Printed in the USA
JSHW020049221221
21446JS00001B/1